Second
reading
11-42 .98

PERRY MASON

IN

The Case of the
Burning Bequest

The New Perry Mason Novels

The Case of Too Many Murders

The Case of the Burning Bequest

PERRY MASON

IN

The Case of the Burning Bequest

by

Thomas Chastain

Based on characters created by
ERLE STANLEY GARDNER

WILLIAM MORROW AND COMPANY, INC.
New York

Recognizing the importance of preserving what has been written, it is the
policy of William Morrow and Company, Inc., and its imprints and affiliates
to have the books it publishes printed on acid-free paper, and we exert our
best efforts to that end.

Printed in the United States of America

BOOK DESIGN BY KATHRYN PARISE

Quality Printing & Binding by:
R.R. Donnelley & Sons Company
1009 Sloan Street
Crawfordsville, IN 47933 U.S.A.

PERRY MASON

IN

The Case of the Burning Bequest

Della Street tapped on the door to Perry Mason's office and went in.

Mason, standing at the desk, had his hat and coat on. He was putting papers into his briefcase.

Della said, "Here are the contracts you gave me to type up. Do you have anything else, Chief?"

"No. That's it for the day, Della." He put the contracts into his briefcase. "You and Gertie can close up. I'm leaving myself."

The phone on Mason's desk rang.

Della reached across and picked up the phone.

"Perry Mason's office."

She listened briefly, then said, "Just a moment, please. I'll see if Mr. Mason's available."

Della put her hand over the mouthpiece of the phone. She looked at Mason.

"A woman. Sounds distraught. She says you don't know her, but that it's urgent she speak with you."

Mason frowned. But as Della knew he would if he thought someone was in trouble and needed his help, he took the phone from her hand.

"Perry Mason speaking."

"Mr. Mason!" The words were rushed. "I'm so glad I reached you! I—we need help. Immediately! There's been a murder—"

"Hold on!" Mason said sharply. "Give me your name and address. Then start at the beginning and tell me about the murder."

Della Street, listening to the one-sided phone conversation, raised her eyebrows as she glanced at Mason when he spoke the word "murder."

The woman on the telephone said, "I—my name is Anne Kimbro. My address is Forty-one Twelve Yordon Drive. That's in Beverly Hills."

Mason made a note of the name and address. "All right, tell me about the murder."

"Yes." There was a pause. "I just called my fiancé. He's at the house we're renovating in Coldwater Canyon. He was frantic. He said he'd just arrived there. He said my stepmother—she was there and somebody had stabbed her to death. He found her like that. Nobody else was there."

"Had he notified the police?"

"I asked him that. He said he had. He said they were on the way. That's why we thought I should call a lawyer for him."

"You and he felt he needed a lawyer?" Mason asked.

"Yes."

"Why?"

Her answer came reluctantly: "He, well, he and my

stepmother didn't get along. She was opposed to our marriage, and they'd had words."

Mason said, "He should have a lawyer there when he talks to the police."

"You will represent him, then?"

"At least until we can find out what this is all about," Mason said. "Give me his name, give me the address of the house." He jotted them down, then added, "Call him back. Tell him I'm on the way. Tell him to advise the police he won't answer any questions until I'm present."

Mason hung up the phone. He put into his briefcase the sheet of paper on which he had noted the name, John Leland, and the address in Coldwater Canyon.

He snapped the briefcase shut as Della asked, "Do we have a new client?"

Mason headed out of the office. "I'll let you know after I've talked to him, and to the police."

The sun was low in the sky to the west as Mason drove out Ventura Boulevard toward Coldwater Canyon. When he reached the foot of the canyon, he turned off Ventura Boulevard and onto the winding road that led upward through the trees and foliage that lined either side of the pavement. Here and there, a house and grounds could be seen from the car, but most of the places were hidden behind walls and hedges, with only mailboxes alongside the canyon road to mark the entrances to the private driveways leading to the secluded residences beyond.

Mason drove slowly, checking the names on the mailboxes, when, as the woman on the phone had instructed him, he neared the top of the canyon. A quarter of a mile on he spotted the name A. KIMBRO on a mailbox set in front of one of a pair of redwood gateposts, and he turned into the blacktop driveway. The driveway wound through more trees and foliage, and ended in a cleared semicircle of lawn. There sat a large colonial-style house, impressive in size but weathered and in need of repairs. Its once-white exterior was faded and discolored, and several windows on the second—top—floor were boarded over.

Two police cars were parked near the entrance to the house, and three other cars, one behind the other, were in the driveway at the side of the house. A uniformed patrolman stood at the front door to the house.

Mason parked his car in the side driveway and got out. He walked toward the patrolman standing guard and nodded.

"I'm Perry Mason, an attorney—"

"Yes, sir," the patrolman said quickly. "We've been expecting you."

Mason followed the patrolman into the house and down a long central hallway to what looked like a glassed-in sunroom at the rear of the house.

There were five men waiting there. Three of them were uniformed patrolmen. Mason supposed he shouldn't be surprised that the fourth man, Lieutenant Ray Dallas, headquarters Homicide Division of the Los Angeles Police Department, was already on the scene. Mason assumed the other man, whom he had never seen before, was his possible new client, John Leland.

The body lay in a far corner of the room near a stone fireplace. The dead woman lay on her side facing away from Mason. The blades of a pair of garden shears had been driven into the center of her back between the shoulders.

Mason looked away from the body and saw that Lieutenant Dallas was watching him.

Dallas said, "Well, now, Counselor, if you're satisfied the victim's dead, could you instruct your client to talk to us, so we can get on with our murder investigation?"

Dallas and Mason were longtime friendly adversaries, one on the side of the prosecution, the other on the side of the defense, in criminal cases, with a bond of mutual respect between them.

"I'd like a word with him in private first," Mason said.

"By all means, do," Dallas said dryly. "We've read him his rights, although judging by the speed with which you arrived, he apparently already knew them."

John Leland, who had been sitting in the only chair in the room, stood as Mason moved toward him and introduced himself.

Leland stuck out his hand and said, "Thank you for coming on such short notice, Mr. Mason. I really didn't know what I should do. I've never been in a situation like this before. When Anne called me, she and I agreed I probably ought to have a lawyer here. Anne says you're the best there is."

Mason was studying the young man as he spoke. Leland appeared very forthright in manner, displaying only a slight air of nervousness, which Mason felt was not all that unusual under the circumstances. His handshake was firm, Mason noted, and his gaze was steady as he waited for Mason to speak. He was, Mason judged, in his late twenties or early thirties. His hair was dark; he was of medium height and weight and had a face with good, strong bones. His left hand had a blood-soaked handkerchief wrapped around it.

"What happened to your hand?" Mason asked.

Leland pointed. "The door from outside. I had to break the glass. It was the only way I could get in."

Mason saw that a pane of glass had been broken in the door leading from the side yard into the sunroom. Pieces of glass lay on the floor.

"Do you need a doctor to look at your hand?" Mason asked.

Leland touched the handkerchief bandage lightly with the fingers of his right hand and grimaced. "Later. I think the worst of the bleeding's stopped. Let's get through here first."

Mason saw that the patrolmen had left the room except for one man standing in the doorway to the hall. Lieutenant Dallas was on the opposite side of the room, talking on the phone.

Mason motioned Leland into the chair. "Tell me what happened from the time you arrived here."

Leland said, "First I want you to know that I didn't answer any questions the police asked me. I told them I wouldn't talk until you were here. Anyhow, I was supposed to meet Anne here—we were going to do some work on the house." He paused and asked, "Did she tell you we're renovating the place?"

"Yes. Go on."

Leland said, "Anne was supposed to be here early, before me, but just before I left the office, Anne phoned me and said she'd be late meeting me, but that I should come on and she'd join me as soon as she could."

Leland's brow was wrinkled as he continued, "When I got here, I saw that there was a car in the driveway. I didn't realize, or recognize, that it was Iris's car."

Mason interrupted, "Iris being the victim?"

"Yes, of course." Leland nodded. "Iris Jantzen, Anne's stepmother."

"You had a key to the house, I assume?"

Leland nodded again. "But when I tried the key, the front door wouldn't open. The door has a deadbolt lock on the inside. I pounded on the door, and when there was no answer, I went around to the side of the house to see if I could get in the door to the sunroom. That door, too, was locked, and I don't have a key to it. But through the glass in the door I could see someone, a body, lying on the floor inside."

Leland paused, touched the handkerchief wrapped around his left hand, and swallowed hard before he said, "My first thought was that it was Anne lying there. That something had happened to her. I didn't even stop to think before I smashed in the glass with my fist, opened the door from the inside, and came in."

Mason nodded encouragingly.

Leland said, "I saw it wasn't Anne lying there. I was relieved, thankful, but at the same time I knew I might be in a jam—under the circumstances."

Mason wanted to hear the explanation from Leland himself. "Why was that?"

"Because everybody knew Iris didn't want Anne and me to get married. She was often bitter about it. And—and here she was dead, and here I was with her body. I thought, naturally, it would look like I killed her."

Mason put his question softly. "Did you think of just leaving, going away, without calling the police?"

Leland hesitated before he nodded reluctantly. "The thought crossed my mind. But then I decided that would be the worst thing I could do. If I ran away and later it could be proved I was here, I thought it would appear for certain I'd killed her. So I called the police."

"You were right to do what you did," Mason agreed. "And you saw no signs of anyone else here, no signs anyone else had been here?"

Leland shook his head.

"Is there anything else?" Mason asked. "Anything you've left out? Think now, before the police start questioning you."

"I—" Leland started to say something, then stopped. He shook his head again.

For the first time Mason believed Leland was being evasive.

"All right, then," Mason said slowly. "The lieutenant will be the one who questions you. I'll step in if he asks anything I don't think you should answer. Otherwise, tell him what you've told me."

Lieutenant Dallas had finished talking on the phone. Mason waved him over, saying, "Mr. Leland's ready to talk to you, Lieutenant."

Lieutenant Dallas took a notebook and a pen from his coat pocket.

John Leland repeated the story he had told Mason. Dallas took notes from time to time, but did not interrupt with questions until Leland completed his account of what had transpired from the time he got to the house until the police arrived.

Dallas said then, "You say the victim, Iris Jantzen, was opposed to your marriage to her stepdaughter, your fiancée, that right?"

"Yes."

"Would she, Iris Jantzen, have known you were going to be here at the house today?"

"I don't know that she would have known. But it's possible. Anne could have told her, I suppose."

Dallas frowned. "And if she had known, doesn't it strike you as odd that she would have come here? If I understand correctly from you, the two of you weren't exactly friends."

"I hadn't thought about it," Leland said. "But, yes, it would be odd."

"Or maybe," Dallas suggested, "she wanted to see you,

to talk to you alone. Can you think of anything she might have wanted to discuss with you in private?"

"Hold on a minute, Lieutenant," Mason interjected. "We don't know that Iris Jantzen was aware that Mr. Leland would be here by himself. Up until the last minute before he left his office, he says he thought his fiancée was to meet him here."

Leland said, "That's true, Lieutenant."

Dallas ran a hand across the top of his graying hair and fixed Leland with a probing stare. "Let's just suppose she did know you were going to be here alone, can you think of any reason she might have to want to see you?"

"I'm sorry, Lieutenant," Mason said quietly, "but I think that's an improper question. You're asking Mr. Leland to conjecture about a matter of which, he has indicated, he has no knowledge."

Ray Dallas shrugged. "Okay. It was just something I had wondered about. We can put it aside for now."

While Dallas had been interrogating Leland, the medical examiner, who had been called earlier, arrived along with a forensic team who would collect fingerprints and other possible evidence at the scene of the crime. A couple of other plainclothesmen were there, too. Mason recognized them as homicide detectives from the headquarters squad.

"Is there anything else, Lieutenant?" Mason asked.

Dallas said, "Not for now."

"I would like Mr. Leland to get to a doctor and have his hand looked after."

The lieutenant looked closely at Leland's bandaged hand. "Are you in any pain, Mr. Leland?"

Leland shook his head.

"Think you can sit tight for a while longer until I've

conferred with the medical examiner? Just in case I have any more questions."

Leland looked at Mason. Mason said, "It's up to you, Mr. Leland."

"I can wait."

"Good," Dallas said, and walked away.

Leland asked, "What happens now, Mr. Mason?"

Mason put a hand on Leland's shoulder. "Just try to relax. I want to see what the medical examiner has to say."

Dallas, the two detectives, and the medical examiner were standing on either side of the body, talking.

Mason walked toward them, stopping a few feet away so he wouldn't be eavesdropping. He looked at the body of the victim. Now that he could see her face, he speculated that she had been in her forties. Her hair was light brown, and she had known enough to use the proper lipstick, eye shadow, and other makeup to make her otherwise-plain face more attractive. Mason stood waiting until Dallas joined him.

"The M.E.'s preliminary examination of the body fixes the time of death as anywhere up to a couple of hours ago," the lieutenant said. "Which doesn't do much to help your client's case."

Mason nodded agreeably. "I can't see where it hurts it, either, Ray. Anyone could have been here, killed her, and left within that time, and before Leland arrived here."

"There's something else, too, Counselor."

Dallas made a motion with his hand, and Mason followed him to a spot near the door leading in from the side yard. There was a small wheelbarrow there, a lawn mower, and some garden tools.

The lieutenant pointed to a single cloth gardener's glove lying under the wheelbarrow.

"One glove," he said. "The forensic guys can't find its mate. You'll notice it's the left glove that's missing."

"And," Mason said, "you're going to tell me that John Leland is apparently left-handed, since that's the hand he used to break in the glass. Which proves what?"

Dallas tilted his head to one side. "That there are going to be no prints on the garden shears that killed the victim, I'll lay odds, because the murderer put on the glove that's missing before he picked up the shears and stabbed her and blood got on the glove."

"And then he disposed of the glove?"

Dallas nodded. "That's what I speculate happened."

"Come on, Ray!" Mason said. "Do you really think Leland would be so stupid as to dispose of only one glove if it would point to his guilt? Why wouldn't he get rid of both gloves, and nobody would even know there were any gloves around in the first place?"

"Because in his panic he didn't think of that," Dallas answered.

Mason shrugged. "I think you're wrong. That glove could have been lost long ago." He took a couple of paces forward, and then turned back. "Anyhow, I don't see how you can overlook one big factor in Leland's favor; he didn't run. He stayed here, after he discovered the body, and he called the police. Does that sound like something a guilty person would do, especially if he was panicked?"

"We'll see," Dallas said. He was looking past Mason, toward the door from the hall. His eyes had narrowed. "Now who's that?"

Mason turned and saw the girl who had just come into the sunroom and was headed directly across to where Leland was sitting in the chair. Leland stood, and they embraced.

"I expect that's the fiancée," Mason said. "Anne Kimbro."

"She sure is some looker," Dallas said.

Mason thought so, too; the girl was slim but nicely proportioned. In high heels she was about the same height as Leland. Her hair was ash-blond, parted on the side, framing a pretty face, the skin of her face dusted with a light suntan.

She and Leland spoke briefly, and then he brought her over and introduced her—"This is Anne Kimbro"— to Mason and Dallas. Up close, Mason could see that her eyes were a sea-green color and that she was young, in her twenties.

"This is a terrible, terrible tragedy," she said, glancing away somberly at the body of her stepmother. "Poor, poor Iris. Who would want to kill her?"

She shook her head and gripped Leland's right hand.

"Do you have any information that might help us in the investigation?" Dallas asked.

"John's told me what he told you," Anne Kimbro said. "I can't think of anything to add. At least not offhand."

Dallas nodded. "I will want to talk to you again."

"Of course."

Mason said quickly, "Lieutenant, if you're finished for now, I think Mr. Leland should get to a doctor."

"I'll drive him," Anne said.

Mason said, "If you have any other questions to ask Mr. Leland, Lieutenant, I'm sure he'll be willing to answer them in the morning."

"Yes, all right," Dallas said. He looked at Leland. "But I want a signed statement from you. Tomorrow at nine A.M. at police headquarters." Dallas paused before he said, "I don't suppose I have to remind you not to leave town meanwhile."

"No, sir."

Mason walked with Leland and Anne to the door of the room. He said to Leland, "Meet me at my office at eight A.M." He gave Leland one of his business cards. "I want to go with you when you make your statement."

After Leland and Anne left, Mason saw that the police were finishing up their work in the room. A couple of morgue attendants who had been called to the house were leaving with the body. The medical examiner went out with them. The forensic team and the two plainclothes detectives, after conferring with Lieutenant Dallas, also left. Dallas posted two uniformed patrolmen to stand watch at the crime scene, and then he and Mason walked to their cars outside.

Dallas said, "I take it, Counselor, that you don't recognize this place?"

Mason was puzzled. "Should I? I don't follow you, Ray."

Dallas turned and looked back at the house, now dark in the early evening except for the lighted front doorway. "The murder tonight isn't the first one to have occurred here. Remember the Larner-Jantzen case? Happened about twenty years ago. A big sensation at the time. It involved murder, money, and sex. The newspapers had a field day with the story."

"I recall something." Mason nodded. "But the details are vague now."

"They would be to me, too, except that about six months ago one of the Sunday papers did a rehash of the case. I happened to read the story. Afterward, out of curiosity I went back and read the police files on it."

"Something about a married woman and her lover, wasn't it?"

Dallas pointed. "The lover shot her right in that house.

She was trying to break off the affair, after her husband found out about it, and her lover killed her. A guy named Edward Larner was the lover, the wife's name was Elizabeth Jantzen. Larner shot her, left her there dead, and took off. There's never been an arrest in the case."

"I'm waiting for the punch line, Ray. What was the relationship of Elizabeth Jantzen to tonight's victim, Iris Jantzen?"

"They were both married to the same guy," Dallas said. "Benjamin Jantzen. One was the first wife, the other the second."

"Let me see if I have this straight, Ray. If that's the case, not only was Iris Jantzen Anne Kimbro's stepparent, but so is Benjamin Jantzen."

"Apparently. According to the investigation of the first murder, as I recall, Elizabeth Jantzen had a child from a previous marriage; the child being, I assume, Anne Kimbro. After the murder her guardian—I assume it's Jantzen—would have had Anne's name legally changed from Kincaid, her father's real name, because the Kincaid name naturally was used in all the sensational stories about the case. There was a lot of stuff involved in that first case. Wealth, contested wills, lawsuits, counterlawsuits."

Dallas paused, then said, "There was something else, too. Elizabeth Jantzen's husband, who died, and her lover, Edward Larner, founded what is still today one of the country's largest pharmaceutical companies, Questall. Larner was a widower at the time of his affair with Elizabeth. The two had known one another for years. And Benjamin Jantzen was, and may still be, an officer with Questall Pharmaceuticals."

Mason said, "Interesting. At the very least I should think all of this would work in young Leland's favor."

Dallas shook his head in amusement. "Never miss a chance to rally to the defense of your client, eh, Counselor? If it's any satisfaction to you, you can be sure I intend to take another look at the files on the first murder."

Mason said, "It strikes me as a peculiar coincidence that both victims were married to the same man and both were killed in the same place."

"I gather you're suggesting the husband would seem the most likely suspect?"

Mason nodded.

"Sorry to have to shoot holes in your speculation," Dallas said. "But you see, it would have been impossible for Benjamin Jantzen to have gotten out here today and to have killed his wife."

"Why's that, Ray?"

"He's been confined to a wheelchair for twenty years after suffering a series of strokes."

Dallas grinned and patted Mason's shoulder. "Stick to your law books, Perry. Leave the detecting to me."

2

Perry Mason got to his office a few minutes before eight the next morning.

Della Street was already there. Mason could tell by the look on her face that something was wrong even before she spoke.

"I've been here about five minutes," Della said, "and Lieutenant Dallas has already called twice. He wants you to call him."

Della followed Mason into his office and took his briefcase.

"All right, Della, I'll call him."

Mason sat down in his comfortable, creaking swivel chair and reached for the phone just as it rang. He answered.

"Mason speaking."

There was none of the friendliness of the night before in Lieutenant Dallas's voice.

"What kind of tricks are you up to, Mason?"

"What are you talking about, Lieutenant?"

"You know what I'm talking about. Where's your client? Where did Leland skip to?"

"Slow down," Mason said. "If you want answers to your questions, it would help if I knew what this was all about. The last time I saw or spoke to Leland was when I was with you."

"He's gone," Dallas said. "We went to his apartment early this morning. He's missing. So are most of his clothes, and his car."

"This is all news to me."

"I had to make sure," Dallas said gruffly.

Mason said, "May I ask why you went to his apartment looking for him this morning? As I recall, you instructed him to be at headquarters at nine A.M.; it's not that time yet."

"I went looking for him at the orders of the D.A."

"Carter Phillips? Why?"

There was a weariness to the lieutenant's voice. "I guess the members of the Jantzen family carry a certain weight with certain parties. Somebody in the family called somebody who called Carter Phillips, demanding to know why I hadn't brought Leland in directly from the scene of the crime and grilled him, if not charged him with murder."

"Did you explain that you'd questioned him last night?" Mason asked.

"I explained. The explanation wasn't good enough for the D.A. He got me out of bed, got a judge out of bed, and got a search warrant issued. I went to Leland's apartment, and the manager of the building let us into the apartment. Among other items, we recovered the shirt Leland was wearing when he was with the victim and his bloodied handkerchief. Phillips wanted the lab people to run a DNA profile on the blood type, or types, on the handkerchief and on the shirt as well, if any traces of blood were found on it."

Mason said, "Look here, Ray, Leland could have spent the night with his fiancée, Anne Kimbro."

"We tried her place," Dallas said. "She was there; he wasn't. She said after the doctor fixed up Leland's hand, she took him to his apartment. She swore she didn't know where he was."

Mason shook his head in exasperation. He said into the phone, "I don't know what to tell you, Ray. Except if I hear from him or see him, I'll produce him for you."

Mason hung up the phone, frowning.

Della had left the office while he had been talking to Ray Dallas. Now, there was a tap on the door, and she came in again. She was carrying a square package.

She said, "A messenger just brought this. It's addressed to you, and it's marked 'Urgent!'"

She put the package, which was enclosed in brown wrapping paper, on Mason's desk. A white envelope addressed to Mason was Scotch-taped to the top of the package.

Mason opened the envelope and took out the handwritten note inside:

The note read:

Dear Mr. Mason—

By the time you receive the tape I have recorded that is inside this package, you will have known that I have not appeared at your office this morning. I hope, after you have listened to what I have to say on the tape, you will understand why. When I think you have had time to listen to the tape, I will phone you. I trust you not to tell anyone else about the contents of the tape until you and I have talked.

Sincerely yours,
J. L.

Mason opened the package and removed a small, book-size tape recorder. He saw that a tape was already in place, ready to play.

Della gathered up the wrapping paper from the desk and went out, closing the door behind her.

Mason switched on the tape recorder and sat back in his chair.

There was no mistaking Leland's voice:

Some years ago there was a murder here in Los Angeles. A man named Edward Larner shot and killed a married woman named Elizabeth Jantzen. It was said that they were lovers, and that she was trying to end their relationship. Her body was found, but the man was never caught. I was five years old at the time. The man, Edward Larner, was my father. My mother had died a year earlier. I went to live with my aunt, my mother's sister. She raised me, and in time we had my name legally changed to John Leland. After I graduated from UCLA, I went to work for my uncle in his real estate office. A couple of years ago my uncle retired, and I took over the office, John Leland, Realtor, as it's now called, in Culver City. No one ever connected me to my father. Approximately three months ago I came back from showing a client a house, and my secretary, Ginny Rollins, told me there had been a message left for me to come to an address in Coldwater Canyon where the owner of a house wanted to talk to me about selling the property. When I went to the address, I met the young woman who owned the house. She was working in the yard, trying to fix up the place. She told me she hadn't called me, and that there must have been a mixup of the address. I was very much attracted to this young woman, and I could tell she liked me. She told me her name was Anne Kimbro, and I told her my name. That day she was just finishing up working on the yard, and on an impulse I asked her to have dinner with me that night, and she accepted. After that we started seeing one another regularly, and, well, we fell in love. It was a while before I met her family. When I heard her stepfather's name, Jantzen, I couldn't believe there could be a connection to the long-ago murder. But there was, of course. Anne Kimbro's mother, who had been Elizabeth Kincaid before she married Benjamin Jantzen, was the woman my father had killed. Anne's last name had been changed, just as mine had, because of the notoriety of the murder. I hadn't thought of my father or the murder in years. I told my aunt what I had discovered, but I couldn't bring myself to tell Anne, or anyone else. But you have to believe me that I had planned to tell Anne before we got married. I was just waiting for the right time. Then, when we announced to Anne's family that we planned to marry, her stepmother, Iris, made it clear that she was opposed to the marriage. From that time on she tried everything she could to break us up, which only made it more difficult for me to tell anyone about who my father was. I was afraid that Iris's opposition to me plus the truth of who I was would be more than Anne could accept, and I'd lose her. I did not kill Iris Jantzen, and I do not know who did kill her, but once people know who I really am, I'm sure no one will believe me. I wanted to tell the whole story, and I needed time to think. I don't know what I should do. . . .

The tape ended there. Mason switched off the recorder. He used the office intercom to call Della Street.

"Della, phone Paul. Tell him I'd like to see him right away. When he gets here, you come in, too; I want you to hear what I have to say."

Mason removed the tape and recorder from his desk and locked them away in a bottom drawer.

He glanced at the morning newspaper Della had put on his desk. There was a front-page story of the murder of Iris Jantzen. The account was brief, and John Leland was reported as having discovered the body. Mason knew that more of the details involved in the case would be carried in later news accounts. He folded the paper away when Della came in, followed by Paul Drake, Jr. The Drake Detective Agency was just down the corridor from Mason's office in the Brill Building. Paul Drake, Jr., had taken over the agency when his father, who had worked for Mason as a private investigator for years, had retired.

"Good morning, Paul," Mason said. "I have a job for you." Drake nodded as he took the big client's chair in front of the desk. Della sat in a chair at the side of the desk, notebook and pen in her hand.

Drake said, "All right, Perry, let's hear it."

Mason related all the events of the night before, including his conversation with Lieutenant Dallas about the twenty-year-old Larner-Jantzen murder case and the phone call from the lieutenant that morning reporting the disappearance of John Leland. He did not mention the tape recording he'd received from Leland that he had locked away in his desk drawer. He felt he should speak to Leland before he disclosed to anyone the confidential information on the tape.

"I don't know, Perry," Drake said slowly when Mason had finished his account. "I'd say we sure have our work cut out for us if we're going to clear Leland of the murder.

It sounds to me like the police have him—if you'll excuse the pun—red-handed."

Mason nodded agreeably, but what he said was, "All the more reason why he needs the best defense he can get. And we're going to see to it that he gets it."

Mason drummed his fingers on the desk. "What I want is all the information we can gather on the Jantzens, the husband, Benjamin, the deceased wife, Iris, and on Anne Kimbro. Also, I want to know everything we can find out about that pharmaceutical company, Questall. All of that's your job, Paul. Use some extra men, if you need them."

Mason swung around in his chair. "And, Della, I want you to go to the library and dig out the microfilm records of the news accounts on the Larner-Jantzen murder case of twenty years or so back. Ray Dallas says it was a sensational story at the time, so there should be plenty of material in the files. Get me copies of as much as you can find."

"Got it," Drake said.

Della nodded. She followed Drake out of the room, and almost immediately used the office intercom to tell Mason, "Chief, Anne Kimbro just came in. There's a man with her. She asked if she could see you."

"You go on to the library, Della. I'll go out and take care of Anne Kimbro."

Mason left his office, leaving the door open.

Anne Kimbro was pacing up and down in the reception area. The man with her was leaning against the wall, his arms folded.

Anne smiled warmly as Mason reached and took her hand.

She said, "Mr. Mason, I'm sorry to come barging in on you like this, but I'm so worried about John."

"Perfectly understandable," Mason assured her.

She turned. "Mr. Mason, this is Neal Granin, Iris's brother. He's a part of our family."

Granin shook hands with Mason. "This is a real pleasure, Mr. Mason. John Leland's lucky to have you in his corner."

"I expect that remains to be seen," Mason said.

Neal Granin was tall, in his early thirties, Mason judged, his hair a reddish-brown. The tortoiseshell glasses he wore gave his face a scholarly look.

Anne said, "Neal, you don't mind waiting while I have a word alone with Mr. Mason?"

Granin smiled. "Not at all."

Mason escorted Anne into his office and closed the door. He waited until she was seated in the client's chair before he went to his desk. "Lieutenant Dallas told me he visited you this morning, looking for Leland."

Anne caught her lower lip between her teeth. "The lieutenant indicated to me that you might have some information as to John's whereabouts."

Mason shook his head. "I'm afraid not. I *am* hoping he'll call me." He leaned forward. "Lieutenant Dallas tells me you said you took Leland home last night, and that's the last you saw of him."

"Took him home isn't exactly accurate," she said. "First, I took him to the doctor, who put a couple of stitches in his hand. Then we drove back to the house in the canyon so John could get his car. I followed him back to his apartment in my car. We said good night, and he went in."

"And you've had no further word from him?"

"None," she said. "I hope he's all right."

"I expect he's just worried about all that's happened and thought he needed a bit of time alone to work things out in his mind." Mason tried to appear reassuring. "It's not an uncommon reaction in such a situation. He impressed me as a very levelheaded young man. I expect he'll be getting in touch with us soon."

Anne smiled wistfully. "On the way to the doctor's John and I talked. He seemed to have such confidence in you. I never expected him to just disappear the way he has."

"Frankly, he hasn't helped his case."

"Surely, he'll see that."

Mason said, "We have to hope so."

She sat forward on the chair. "The police seem to think he had reason to kill Iris because she didn't want me to marry him. That's just nonsense! I'd never let her prevent me from marrying John, no matter what she said. And he knew that!"

Mason smiled. "He's lucky to have such a spirited advocate as you in his corner."

"That reminds me." She opened her handbag and took out a checkbook and pen. She wrote out a check and handed it to him. "Will that be sufficient as a retainer until you work out your fee with John?"

Mason saw that the check was payable in the amount of twenty-five thousand dollars.

He said, "Depending upon what I have to do, it may be more than sufficient, Miss Kimbro."

"Anne, Mr. Mason. Please call me Anne. I want us to be friends."

"I'd like that, too."

She stood. "I'm glad you're working for John. You've been very kind and very helpful."

"Try not to worry too much," Mason said.

When Mason and Anne walked back out to the reception area, Neal Granin said, "Mr. Mason, might I have a word with you, too? I'll only take a few minutes of your time."

"Yes. All right," Mason said.

Granin looked at Anne. "Okay?"

Anne nodded. "I'll wait for you downstairs, in the car."

In Mason's office, with the door closed again, Granin said, "It may seem strange to you that I'm pleased you're working for John Leland; I mean, considering that Iris was my sister and that the police appear to regard him as a possible suspect in her death. The fact is, I like John, and I have trouble believing he had anything to do with the murder."

"I'm glad to hear that," Mason said.

Granin leaned forward in his chair. "However, that's not the reason why I wanted to talk to you. My real concern at the moment is what the family—Mr. Jantzen and, especially, Anne—are going to have to go through as a result of this tragedy." He looked at Mason intently. "You do know, don't you, that this is not the first murder involving a member of the family?"

Mason nodded. "I know. I'm aware of the earlier case."

"It just seems so unfair," Granin said. "Because you know and I know the newspapers and TV are going to rehash the scandalous details of that story now that Iris, too, has been murdered."

Mason agreed. "Most likely they will. I'm afraid there's not much anyone can do about that. It'll make good copy. And it makes no difference that, at this point, as far as anyone knows, your sister could have been killed by random chance—by a prowler or a burglar."

"Exactly," Granin said. "And it seems a terrible shame that Anne and Ben Jantzen are going to have to endure having the whole world be reminded of Anne's real mother's murder years ago."

"I can appreciate your feelings," Mason said. "And I can tell you that I have no plans at the moment of making any public statements about the earlier case simply to divert suspicion away from John Leland." Mason grinned. "I expect that's what you really wanted to hear from me."

Granin smiled sheepishly. "Something like that, yes."

He stood and shook hands with Mason. "Thank you for giving me a hearing."

Granin left the office.

Gertie, the receptionist who also operated the switchboard in the outer office, called in on the intercom, "Mr. Mason, I'm holding a call for you from a party who says he wants to talk to you about a package he sent you. He asked me not to tell you he was on the line until you were alone."

Mason reached for the phone. "I've been expecting the call, Gertie. Put him through."

As soon as he heard John Leland's voice, Mason said brusquely, "Listen to me carefully, Leland. You've made a foolish mistake in running away. I think we can still set things straight, but we have to talk. And I mean right away! Tell me where you are, and I'll come there."

"I'm in Santa Monica," Leland said. "A motel."

Mason wrote down the address and ended the conversation, "Stay there!"

3

John Leland opened the door to the motel room. "Come in, Mr. Mason."

Leland looked drawn and disheveled. His eyes were bloodshot, and he needed a shave. There was a bandage on his left hand. His clothes were rumpled, as if he'd slept in them, and if he had, Mason thought, he'd slept on top of the bedspread with a thin blanket, which was thrown back to one side of the bed, over him. A couple of suitcases and a carryall, all unopened, sat in a corner of the room.

Mason sat in the only armchair in the room. He didn't take off his hat or the light raincoat he had on, his hands thrust deep into the raincoat's pocket. Leland sat on the bed.

Mason said, "If you want me to help you, you're going to do exactly what I tell you to do from now on. Understand?"

"I understand. Yes. But can you help me? Now that you know who I really am."

Mason ignored the question. "Last night I asked you if there was anything you hadn't told me. You said there wasn't. This morning I find out there's a whole lot you hadn't told me."

Leland tried to explain. "I didn't want to tell anybody about my father until I had told Anne first. Last night I thought I'd be able to tell her when she drove me to the doctor's, and we were alone. Then I found out I just couldn't do it. I was afraid she'd hate me, and I'd lose her. . . ."

"And what did you think you'd gain by running away?"

"I didn't think. That was the trouble, Mr. Mason. After several hours here alone, I realized there was nothing I could do except tell the whole story; face the truth no matter how guilty it made me look." His shoulders slumped, and he wiped his hand across his face. "Last night I bought the tape recorder, and early this morning I drove into L.A. and took it to a messenger service to be delivered to you."

"And there are no other surprises I should know about?" Mason demanded.

Leland shook his head miserably. "No."

Mason pushed his hat back on his head. "All right then, let's get busy and try to repair the damage you've done to your case so far. Now, I want you to shave and change your clothes. Then we're going in and talk to Lieutenant Dallas. You're going to tell him everything you told me on the tape."

"But what about Anne? I don't want her to hear all that stuff from somebody else."

"You'll talk to the lieutenant first. I'll make arrangements, however, for you to see her as soon as you're finished with him. Get moving."

Leland took one of his suitcases and went into the bathroom.

Mason phoned Anne Kimbro. He told her he expected to be at police headquarters in about an hour. He asked her to meet him there, and he cautioned her not to talk to anyone until he saw her. She said she'd be there and he thought, *Good girl*, when he hung up the phone; she hadn't asked him any questions.

When Leland came back into the room, shaved and dressed in different clothes, he asked, "What happens now?"

Mason was standing at the window, looking out. He said, "On my way here I phoned a private investigator who works for me, Paul Drake, Jr. I left a message for him to bring one of his operatives and meet us here. His office will have located him by now, and he should be here any minute. I want you to drive to headquarters with me. The man Drake brings here will drive your car, with your luggage, to your apartment and leave everything there, and Drake will pick him up."

Leland was frowning. "Wouldn't it be simpler for me to drive my own car to headquarters, with you following me?"

Mason shook his head. "We can't risk it. Dallas may have an APB—all-points bulletin—out on you and your car, with orders to pick you up. I don't want that to happen. I want you to go in with me voluntarily, for questioning."

Leland looked puzzled. "Would the police do that? Pick me up? I'm not exactly a fugitive. I wasn't arrested."

"They can pick you up on a material-witness charge."

Mason looked around from the window. "Earlier this morning the police got a search warrant and went to your apartment. Dallas knows you packed up some things and left. They've been trying to locate you ever since. They can pick you up all right."

"Does Anne know all this?"

"Yes," Mason said. "They went to her place, looking for you. And she came to see me this morning before you phoned me. I didn't mention your tape recording."

Mason looked back out the window. "Incidentally, she gave me a check for twenty-five-thousand dollars as a retainer for representing you."

"She didn't have to do that," Leland said sadly. "I have plenty of money. You and I just hadn't had a chance to discuss your fee."

"Let's don't worry about that now. You can pay her back, or pay me once we see what happens to you."

"What do you think is going to happen to me? I mean once I've talked to Lieutenant Dallas."

Mason said, "I can't answer that yet. Dallas didn't have enough evidence, physical evidence, to arrest you last night. The police will want more physical evidence, I believe, before they would take the step of formally charging you. That was the reason they got a search warrant and went to your apartment."

"What were they looking for?" Leland asked.

"Any physical evidence they could find that would link you to the murder. One thing they did take, so Dallas told me, was the shirt you were wearing last night. And the handkerchief you used as a bandage."

Leland came over and stood beside Mason at the window. "They saw my shirt last night. Why do they want it now? And the handkerchief?"

Mason said, "They want to test for blood types. Specifically, to see if they can find any traces of Iris Jantzen's blood."

Leland looked worried. "But there might be. It's possible I got some of her blood on the shirt or my handkerchief when I first broke into the sunroom and thought the body might be Anne's." He paused before he asked, "If they do find Iris's blood on my things, will they arrest me right then? Before I have a chance to try to talk to Anne?"

"I phoned her while you were in the shower," Mason said. "She's going to be at headquarters, so you can see her after you've spoken with Dallas. In any event, if they find any traces of Iris's blood, your blood, or anyone else's, they'll run a DNA profile on the blood, a matter of separating out a genetic pattern from the blood. It's this DNA genetic pattern that can positively identify an individual by a bloodstain, body fluids, small skin samples, even within the root of a single hair left at a scene by either the victim or the assailant. From what I've gathered about this relatively new testing, no two people—except identical twins—have the same DNA in their cells."

Mason pointed out the window and started toward the door. "Here come Drake and his man now."

4

There was silence in the interrogation room at police headquarters when John Leland concluded his statement of all the facts he had revealed earlier on the tape he'd had delivered to Perry Mason that morning.

Mason sat on one side of the long conference table beside Leland. Lieutenant Ray Dallas sat directly opposite Mason. A police stenographer, at the end of the table, had recorded Leland's words. Two plainclothes homicide detectives, McKeevy and Jessup, sat in chairs against the wall behind Dallas. The D.A., Carter Phillips, sat at the head of the table.

Mason ended the silence: "All right, gentlemen, there you have it. A full and frank account from Mr. Leland about information that probably isn't even relevant to the murder of Iris Jantzen. Information, I might add, that

Mr. Leland has voluntarily given you by way of explanation for his delay in appearing here today. He simply needed time to collect his thoughts. And he has shown by his action now and by his statement that he is cooperating with your investigation to the best of his ability."

D.A. Phillips smiled thinly. "That's a nice speech, Mr. Defense Attorney. However, there are a couple of points I'd like to have clarified by Mr. Leland."

Mason nodded. "That's why we're here. Proceed."

Phillips fixed his eyes on Leland. The D.A. was short and stocky. With his thick mane of black hair combed back from a high forehead, he was a man who projected, as he did now, a great deliberateness in speech and gesture as he said, "I'm curious about one thing, Mr. Leland. You say that your office received a phone call about a house for sale in Coldwater Canyon and when you went to the address given, you met Anne Kimbro for the first time. Is that correct?"

Leland answered quickly, "Yes, sir. That's the way it happened."

"Well, my question is, later, when you discovered who Anne Kimbro was, that there was a connection between the two of you, through your father and her mother, did you then, or at any time, attempt to find out the correct address of the house for sale in the canyon?"

Leland frowned. "Did I try to find out the correct address? I can't recall that I did, no, sir. But it's not unusual for people calling the office to get mixed up on addresses. I just assumed that was what happened. I never gave it much thought, truthfully."

Carter Phillips cleared his throat. "I take it then that earlier, before you ever went to that house and met Anne Kimbro, you'd never had any curiosity about seeing the house where the event took place that must surely have been a terrible blight on you all your life?"

Leland shook his head. "I can't recall ever wanting to see the house, no, sir. To tell you the truth, I doubt that I'd have been able to find it if I'd wanted to see it. I mean, all that happened with my father was a closed chapter in my life. I had to make it so."

"I understand that a few months ago there was an article in one of the Sunday newspapers on the case involving your father. Did you happen to see it?"

"No," Leland said.

"And when you met Anne Kimbro for the first time, you didn't know who she was? That her name had been Anne Kincaid before she had it changed to Kimbro?"

Leland shook his head. "How could I know that?"

"You could have looked it up in the court records. Anyone can look up such matters."

"I didn't," Leland insisted. "I had no reason to look it up."

Perry Mason sat quietly listening to the exchange between the D.A. and Leland. So far, Mason was pleased with the way Leland was responding to the interrogation. Mason often had observed that most people had a tendency to overexplain when answering a question. And in overexplaining, people frequently revealed more about themselves than they ever meant to reveal. Experienced lawyers were aware of this, and so were knowledgeable newspaper reporters and, of course, the police. In fact, Mason knew, the police always hoped this would happen during an interrogation, and it was one reason why they prolonged their interrogations and sometimes deliberately repeated the same questions, rephrased in a different manner.

Carter Phillips had paused after his last question and

Leland's answer, scribbled a note on a pad in front of him, and then looked at Ray Dallas. "Do you have any questions for Mr. Leland, Lieutenant?"

Dallas sat up straighter in his chair. "There is one matter I'd like to get clear on, Mr. Leland. Last night you told me you'd arrived at the house at approximately five-fifteen P.M.—"

Leland corrected him. "It was between five-fifteen and five-thirty, I believe I said. Or at least that's what I meant to say—"

Dallas had glanced down at the paper in front of him. He nodded. "So you did. My question, then, is, Did you notice anyone along the way to the house? I mean, any nearby neighbors?"

"No, no, not that I recall."

"No one?"

"No, sir. Not that I can recall."

Dallas, too, made a note on the paper in front of him. "I have no further questions for now."

Mason made a motion as if to rise. "I assume, gentlemen, Mr. Leland is free to leave?"

D.A. Phillips said, "Mr. Mason, I would advise you to admonish your client not to disappear again."

Mason looked directly at Leland. "I already have, Mr. Phillips. Mr. Leland has assured me he realizes he made a mistake this morning that he does not intend to repeat."

"For the record," Phillips said, "I want it noted that I am instructing Mr. Leland that even now he could be held at the very least as a material witness in this case. And that there will undoubtedly be additional questions we may want to ask of him."

"Yes, sir," Leland answered quickly.

Phillips, Dallas, and the two detectives were conferring among themselves as Mason walked with Leland from the interrogation room to the hallway outside.

Leland took a few steps, turned, and asked searchingly, "What were all those questions about, Mr. Mason? I couldn't grasp their significance."

"Nothing you need be too concerned about," Mason reassured him. "D.A. Phillips asked you about the original phone call your office received about the house for sale in Coldwater Canyon because he's trying to find out if there's any way you can verify that such a call was made. If not, he can suggest there was no such call, ever. That you made up the story to explain how you happened to meet Anne. That before you went there, you knew about the house, you knew she'd be there, and that you had some purpose in wanting to meet her."

Leland shook his head. "I didn't understand what the questions were all about. And what was the lieutenant driving at, when he asked about possible nearby neighbors around the house? Asking did I see any?"

Mason said, "That would indicate to me that he plans to make a canvass of the area near there to see if anyone happened to see you on your way to the house. It's part of the routine police investigation of the murder."

Leland shook his head again. "But what if someone did see me—or didn't see me—what's it going to prove?"

Mason's answer was gentle. "That would depend upon what any possible witnesses might have to say. The police won't know that until they've made a canvass of the area."

"What you're really saying is, the police are trying to make a case against me," Leland said slowly.

Mason put a hand on Leland's shoulder. "What I'm really saying is, again, this is routine in a police investigation of a possible suspect in a murder case. Certainly, we can expect them to make similar investigations of other possible suspects as time goes on and more information is developed. And it's my job to make sure they do that."

Mason stopped in front of the door to an office along the hall. "I arranged with Lieutenant Dallas that we could use this office in private, if you want to speak with Anne now."

"She's here?" Leland asked.

"I expect so," Mason said. "I told her to wait inside the front of the building near the booking desk, and I'd bring her to you when we'd finished with your statement." Mason motioned Leland into the office. "Why don't you go on in and wait until I get her?" He looked at Leland. "You do want to see her, don't you?"

"Yes. I know I have to see her, talk to her. I just don't know how she's going to take what I have to tell her."

"I'll be waiting until you've had your talk," Mason said. He left Leland and went on toward the front of the building.

Anne Kimbro was easy to spot, standing near the door to headquarters. She was smartly dressed in a dark jacket and matching skirt, her hair pulled back from her face under a broad-brimmed white straw hat with a dark band that matched her skirt and jacket. She hurried toward Mason as soon as she saw him.

"Is John all right?" she asked anxiously. "Why isn't he with you?"

Mason took her by the arm and walked with her back down the hall. "He's fine. He's waiting to talk to you."

"Can we leave then? Can he leave?"

Mason nodded. "Yes, yes. The police have finished

questioning him. He's free to go. But he wanted to talk to you here, first."

"I knew they couldn't arrest him!" Anne exclaimed excitedly. "Oh, thank you so much for helping him through all this."

"It's not all over yet," Mason said. "There'll be more questions. But we'll deal with them as they come."

They had reached the office where John Leland was waiting in the open doorway. Anne ran to him and threw both her arms around his neck, laughing. Leland swung her around and into the office. Mason gently closed the door on them and walked to the other side of the hallway.

From where he was standing he saw Dallas, D.A. Phillips, and the two detectives come out of the interrogation room. The D.A. and the detectives went off in the opposite direction. Dallas came along the hall toward Mason and, when he reached him, said, "I don't think I'm violating any confidences, Counselor, when I tell you that Carter Phillips is convinced your client's guilty."

"Fair enough," Mason said reasonably. "But he's going to have to prove it."

"I think you should be prepared to expect an indictment to be handed down."

"Even before the lab tests are done on Leland's shirt and handkerchief?"

Dallas shrugged. "Phillips is gung ho to charge Leland. He may not wait. Or he may not think he needs any more evidence."

"The only evidence he has is pretty flimsy and circumstantial," Mason pointed out.

Dallas tugged at an earlobe. "Circumstantial evidence has been known to be enough to sway many a jury. You know that, Counselor, as well as Phillips knows it."

Mason was silent. Dallas looked at the closed door to the office across the hall. "Leland in there with Anne Kimbro?"

"Yes."

Dallas shook his head. "Boy, I wouldn't want to be in his shoes, even if he's innocent. How do you break the news to someone you're about to marry that your father killed her mother?"

Mason saw the office door open. He said, "We should have the answer to that one in just a minute."

Both men watched as Anne Kimbro came out of the office. She held her wide-brimmed hat in one hand, and was wiping tears with the handkerchief she held in her other hand. She didn't seem to notice Mason and Dallas standing in the hall as, head down, she fled down the hall toward the front entrance.

Leland came out of the office slowly, shoulders slumped, his face somber.

"I have to get him out of here, Ray," Mason said.

"Yeah," Dallas said. "He's going to need some consoling, Counselor."

5

Mason had to drive John Leland home after they left police headquarters, since Leland's car had been left at his apartment house by Drake's operative.

Leland was depressed after the talk he'd had with Anne Kimbro. "When I told her who I was, Mr. Mason, she was absolutely shocked," he told Mason sadly. "She couldn't even bring herself to look at me. I don't think she was angry with me so much as that she was shocked. She broke into tears, she wouldn't let me come near her, and then she ran out of the office."

Mason was sympathetic. "I realize her reaction must have made you unhappy. But you know she might feel differently after she's had time to adjust to what had to have been painful news."

Leland was uncertain. "Maybe. But the most terrible part of it was that I felt she felt I had betrayed her somehow. I never meant to, never felt that was what I was doing during the time I didn't tell her who I really was. Now, I don't know if she'll ever love me again."

"I think you'll just have to wait and see."

"Talk about 'the sins of the fathers,' " Leland said bitterly. "All my life I tried not to think about what my father did. I told myself—my aunt, Janine, told me, too, over and over—that whatever had happened with my father had nothing to do with me. And now, here I am, having to suffer for his sins!"

"Yes, for now and to a degree, that's true," Mason agreed. He was silent for a moment before he said, "I haven't asked you this before, John, but have you, has anyone in your family, ever heard any word of your father since he disappeared?"

There was still bitterness in Leland's voice when he answered, "Oh, yes. Or so my aunt told me when I was older. It seems that for a time when I was little, right after the . . . the murder, he sent money from time to time that was to be used to take care of me. Money orders sent from different cities, the envelopes typed, with no return address, no messages, so my aunt said."

"He sent the money to her?"

"To my uncle. Not Janine's husband; my other uncle, my father's brother, Joe Larner. Joe and my father were supposed to have been close before my father went away. Joe worked with him in the company."

Mason asked, "And your uncle, Joe, gave the money to your aunt?"

Leland nodded and said, "But my aunt would never accept the money. She always gave it back to Joe. And Aunt Janine always notified the police when the money orders came, and told them where they were sent from. She told me that after a while the money orders stopped coming. She thought that was because he, my father, caught on that somebody was telling the police about them and about where he might be."

"Do you remember your father?"

"Some." Leland thought for a moment. "I remember that he took me to the baseball games once in a while. And he and my mother and I went to the beach other times. But I never saw him a lot at home, that I can remember. I think he was at work most of the time, even at nights before I was put to bed. I remember more about my mother, before she died. It was after that, I think, that he used to take me to the ball games. The truth is that my aunt Janine and uncle Frank always seemed to be more my parents than my real parents were."

Mason tried to cheer him up. "It appears that you were able to have a stable life with your aunt and uncle, despite the past. And when you did meet Anne Kimbro, she fell in love with you."

They had reached Leland's apartment building, and Mason stopped the car.

Leland was frowning. "Talking about meeting Anne Kimbro, Mr. Mason; do you believe I told the truth about how I came to meet her, since apparently the police don't believe me?"

"I'll tell you what I think," Mason answered directly. "It would have to be a pretty strange coincidence that because someone called your office and gave the wrong address, you'd wind up, after all these years, meeting by chance the daughter of the woman your father killed."

Leland exhaled his breath in frustration. "Then you don't believe me?"

"That's not what I said," Mason answered. "Either you haven't told the truth, or somebody called your office and gave the correct address of the house they said was for sale in order to deliberately lure you into a meeting with Anne."

"But why would anyone do that?"

Mason grinned. "That's part of the puzzle we have to figure out. Be patient."

Leland nodded. "All right. Okay. I'll try."

He shook hands with Mason, and turned to get out of the car.

Mason said, "One more thing, John. You must not consider running off again. No matter what happens. If you are indicted, the court will probably consider that this one time you might have panicked and disappeared briefly, and it won't necessarily be held against you. But if it should happen again and the police catch up with you, or even if you come back on your own, the court will order you to jail and you won't get out again before the trial."

"I understand, Mr. Mason. I assure you I won't run away again. No matter what happens."

Mason drove back to his office.

It was early afternoon. Della Street had returned with an armful of photocopies of microfilm of the twenty-year-old newspaper stories that had appeared at the time of the Larner-Jantzen murder case.

"I think I found everything they wrote about the case," Della told Mason. "Including that story you said Lieutenant Dallas mentioned had run in the Sunday paper about six months ago. I arranged the original accounts in sequence as they appeared, so you'll be able to follow the developments in the case as they were reported. The piece from six months ago is on the bottom of the stack."

"Thank you, Della."

"I read through most of the stories. It was quite a scandal at the time."

"Apparently." Mason nodded.

"Do you think it's possible there's a connection between that murder and the one last night?"

Mason shrugged. "Despite what I frequently say to the contrary, *sometimes* coincidences do happen."

"Well, I think it would be a darn shame if the police have picked our client as the chief suspect in the murder last night because of something his father did years ago."

"I think you'll find that you and I and our client would agree on that."

Della nodded and left the room.

Mason centered the photocopies of the newspaper clippings on his desk and began to read.

Elizabeth Jantzen had first been reported by her husband as a missing person. Three days after that report, her body had been found in the house, still under construction, in Coldwater Canyon. She had been shot in the head by a .38-caliber bullet. No weapon was found at the scene. The body was discovered by Joseph Larner, who had gone to the house looking for his brother, Edward Larner. Edward Larner, believed to be the owner of the house under construction, had not been seen for three days. Police were unable to question Benjamin Jantzen, husband of Elizabeth, who had had a stroke on the day he first had reported his wife missing. Later, a police check disclosed the fact that Edward Larner had a gun permit for a .38-caliber revolver. At that point police issued a warrant for the arrest of Edward Larner as a material witness in the case. No trace could be found of him. In subsequent days it was revealed, through the questioning of those who had been close to Elizabeth Jantzen, and to Edward Larner—including Larner's brother, Joseph—that the two had been having an affair. It was also disclosed that Benjamin Jantzen had learned of the affair, had confronted his wife, and that she had agreed to end her relationship with Edward Larner. Police theorized that Elizabeth Jantzen had gone to see Edward Larner to tell him that the affair was ended and that he had shot and killed her, then fled. Adding to this theory was the fact Edward Larner had transferred the deed to the house he was having constructed to Elizabeth Jantzen. Speculation was that Larner had hoped she would leave her husband and marry him, and they would live together in the new house. News accounts identified Elizabeth Jantzen as the widow of Martin Kincaid, who, with Edward Larner, founded the multibillion-dollar Questall Pharmaceutical Company, prior to her marriage to Benjamin Jantzen. Both Elizabeth and Benjamin were officers of the company, as was Edward Larner. Elizabeth Jantzen was reported to have a daughter from her first marriage, and Edward Larner, a widower, a son.

As Perry read through the clippings, he had to shake his head at the lurid descriptions some of the newspapers used in reporting the case. The murder itself frequently was referred to as "the Scarlet Scandal"; the house described as "the Deadly Love Nest," and "the Honeymoon House of Horror." The victim—because she had been left her first husband's holdings in the pharmaceutical company—was called "the Merry Heiress," Larner "the Spurned Lover," and the husband, Benjamin, "the Superfluous Spouse."

The final story written on the murder twenty years later, which Lieutenant Dallas had read and told Mason about, included the basic facts newspapers had reported at the time, along with additional information about subsequent developments. Edward Larner had never been apprehended. Although the police believed that several times they had come close to catching him, Larner remained a fugitive from justice. Some time after his wife's murder Benjamin Jantzen had married Iris Granin, who had been his wife's social secretary, and in recent years Jantzen had suffered a series of strokes. Some sources were quoted as saying they thought his initial stroke had occurred because when he first found his wife was missing, he thought she had left him and run off with Edward Larner. Mention was made that Elizabeth Jantzen had had a daughter by her first marriage and that Edward Larner had had a son, but neither was identified by name.

Perry Mason put the copies of the newspaper clippings into a file folder and leaned back at the big desk. The expression on his face was like the expression of a mathematician contemplating a complex numerical theorem. The difference was, in Mason's case he had to come up with the right answer to save his client's skin.

6

The next day, in midmorning, Perry Mason left his office and drove out to Culver City. He parked his car across the street from the building where he could see lettered on the front pane-glass window the words JOHN LELAND, REALTOR.

Mason had spoken on the phone with Leland earlier. When Leland mentioned that he would be out for most of the morning with a client, Mason decided it would give him an opportunity to talk alone with Leland's secretary, Ginny Rollins.

He waited in the car until he saw that Leland wasn't in the office, and then he went across the street and entered the building.

The young woman sitting at the typewriter turned and smiled. "Yes, sir? Can I help you?"

"You *are* Ginny Rollins, aren't you? I'm Perry Mason, an attorney—"

"Oh, yes, Mr. Leland told me about you." She stood up and offered her hand.

She was slim, small, dark-haired. Her deep brown eyes were fringed by long black eyelashes. She wore a white silk blouse, black tailored skirt, and black pumps, her look from head to toe neat and tidy.

She said, "You just missed Mr. Leland. He went out to visit a client. I know where to reach him, if you'd like."

Mason smiled. "Actually, it's you I wanted to see, Ms. Rollins. Mr. Leland did tell you I'm representing him, didn't he?"

"Yes, he did. He told me all that's happened—with the police and all, I mean. And that you'd agreed to help him. The police can't seriously believe he could have had anything to do with that poor woman's death, can they?"

"They're just doing their job," Mason said. "And John Leland happens to be a possible suspect."

"Well, they'd better find someone else to suspect!" she said indignantly. She looked at Mason. "*You* don't think he had anything to do with her death, do you?"

"What I think isn't going to make much difference to the police," Mason told her. "My job is to clear him of any possible charges. That's why I want to talk to you."

"I'll help him any way I can," she said quickly. "Just tell me what I can do."

Mason raised a hand. "Not so fast now. All I want you to do is answer truthfully the questions I'm going to ask you. Questions the police will probably be asking you, as well, sooner or later."

She sat down in her chair. "You want to know about that first phone call, when Mr. Leland went out to Coldwater Canyon that first day, don't you? Mr. Leland has already asked me what I remember about it, and how important it could be."

She looked at him searchingly.

Mason nodded. "That's one of my questions, yes. What do you remember?"

"That's a hard question to answer simply."

"It shouldn't be."

"It is, though," she said, frowning. "That is, it's hard to answer, without an explanation, and still be fair to Mr. Leland."

"Then answer it with an explanation," Mason suggested.

She took a deep breath. "To say I don't actually remember the call doesn't mean there wasn't a call. What I mean is, we get tons of calls every day. If Mr. Leland's out, I write the person's name and address or phone number on a message pad"—she paused to show Mason a stack of message pads—"and when Mr. Leland comes in, he takes the page and either returns the call or goes out to see the possible client. You see?"

"And you don't keep a permanent record of the calls?"

She shook her head. "Not unless the possible client becomes a real client. So, by the time Mr. Leland first asked me if I remembered receiving that particular call, a long time had passed. We've had lots of calls from time to time from people who want to buy or sell a house in Coldwater Canyon. There's just no reason why I would remember one such call from another. I want to help Mr. Leland, and I don't understand why anyone wouldn't believe him if he says there was a call, no matter what I do or don't remember."

She looked so distressed that Mason had to pat her on the shoulder, and nod reassuringly.

Before she could say anything else, the phone rang.

She answered, "John Leland, Realtor." Then she said, "Yes. Just a moment," and handed the phone to Mason.

Della Street was calling. "Perry, Paul just phoned in. He wants to know if you can have lunch with him at twelve-thirty at Clay's Bar and Grill. He's going to call back to verify."

Mason glanced at his watch. "Fine, Della. Tell Paul I'll be there."

As Mason handed the phone back to Ginny Rollins, the door to the office opened. Lieutenant Ray Dallas came in, followed by homicide detective Joseph McKeevy.

"Well, well," Dallas said. "Small world, wouldn't you say, Mason?"

"At times, Lieutenant, at times."

Dallas turned toward Ginny Rollins. "And I suppose this is the possible witness we all came to see."

Mason smiled at the secretary. "Ginny Rollins, this is Lieutenant Dallas, Los Angeles Police Department. And Detective McKeevy."

Mason lifted a hand and let it fall. "And now I'll be on my way. Thank you for talking with me, Ms. Rollins."

"Yes," she answered, looking none too happy at the prospect of being interviewed by the police.

Mason would have liked to have stayed to lend her moral support. But he suspected that his presence would only serve to annoy the two detectives and make the interview more difficult for her.

He left the real estate office, closing the door on the lieutenant's words directed to Ginny Rollins: "Just a couple of questions—"

Mason drove back toward downtown L.A. and entered Clay's Bar and Grill a few minutes before twelve-thirty. Drake was already there, sitting at a table, drinking a cup of coffee.

Mason pulled out a chair and sat down. "Tell me you have something for me, Paul. I have a hunch D.A. Phillips is going to spring a murder indictment on our client any moment now."

Drake tilted his chair back. "I have plenty to tell you, Perry. The problem is whether any of it's going to help Leland."

Before Drake could continue, the waiter came to the table, and they ordered lunch.

The waiter went away. Drake said, "I warn you, Perry, the case is a tangled skein of personalities."

Mason nodded. "So I gathered. Della got me all the newspaper accounts on the earlier murder and the family. I read them yesterday."

"What's particularly interesting," Drake said, "is that John Leland's father and Anne Kimbro's mother were star-crossed lovers, and it's as if they've passed that legacy on to their only children."

"You think then that Anne's mother, Elizabeth, really loved Leland's father? Even though she felt she had to end their affair?"

Drake nodded. "From what my sources tell me, Edward Larner and Elizabeth Kincaid were in love even while Larner's wife was alive and Elizabeth was still married to Anne's real father, Martin Kincaid."

Mason frowned. "You mean their affair started that far back? *Before* Larner's wife died and Kincaid died, *before* Elizabeth married Benjamin Jantzen?"

"No, no. According to my information they were in love with one another but they didn't have an affair. Besides, Larner and Kincaid were not only partners in the pharmaceutical company they started together but were best friends."

"So, if I understand correctly," Mason said slowly, "the

affair didn't happen until after Elizabeth married Jantzen."

Drake nodded. "Right. And not even then, not until Larner's wife died."

Mason rubbed his chin reflectively. "If that was the case, after Kincaid died, why didn't Elizabeth wait for Larner, why did she marry Jantzen?"

"The best guess anyone has is that of course Elizabeth didn't know that Larner's wife was going to die. And, apparently, she felt she needed a husband. Benjamin Jantzen was there, a bachelor, a longtime friend, too, and had been a part of the pharmaceutical company from the time it was first formed. Kincaid had left everything to Elizabeth when he died, and don't forget that included his half of the business. There are those who think Elizabeth felt she needed Jantzen's help in running the company, and that that might have been part of the reason she married him when she did."

"What about Elizabeth's share of the company?" Mason asked. "What happened when she was killed?"

"Everything went to Anne, in trust until Anne's twenty-fourth birthday. Jantzen was made executor of the estate."

"And what about Larner's share of the company?"

Drake said, "Most of his estate was left to his son, now John Leland, and there were also provisions made for Larner's brother, Joseph. But because Larner murdered Elizabeth and has been a fugitive ever since, that will has never been executed. Joseph Larner and Benjamin Jantzen and/or Iris Jantzen have been in litigation in the courts for years now, and the matter is still unresolved."

"You're right, Paul," Mason said. "It is a tangled skein."

Drake leaned forward in the chair. "There's one other curious matter of litigation in the case that's also been dragging on for years. Not long after the company, Questall, went into business, there was a big lawsuit against it."

Drake took a notebook from his pocket and glanced at it. "A woman named Clara Newcombe, who had a problem of high blood pressure, is claimed to have had a disabling illness after using one of the products made by Questall. The husband, Bernard Newcombe, brought suit against Questall for millions of dollars. The company withdrew the product from the market. In the first court round the Newcombes won the case. The company appealed, and the decision was reversed. At that point officials of the company began receiving anonymous death threats. They believed the threats to be the work of Bernard Newcombe, but could never prove it."

Mason said, "But if that happened soon after the company went into business, it surely can't have any pertinency to recent events."

Drake grinned and put the notebook away. "There's more, Perry. About two years ago Clara Newcombe committed suicide. The husband, Bernard, claimed it was a result of Questall's medication, years before, and brought suit again. This time the court threw out the suit before it went to trial. And guess what happened?"

"The death threats started up once more?"

Drake grinned again. "You got it. And guess who— because she was more or less running the company since her husband was confined to a wheelchair—was the target of the most recent threats? The recently deceased Iris Jantzen."

"There may be something there." Mason nodded slowly. "Now, tell me about Iris."

Before Drake could answer, the waiter brought the lunches.

After they were served, Drake said, "From what my

investigators and I have been able to discover, the shared opinion about Iris is that she was ambitious, smart, sharp. For most of her life she had a kid brother to support, and apparently the responsibility rested heavily upon her. Everyone says that when she was the first Mrs. Jantzen's social secretary, she did almost everything for her. When Elizabeth was killed, I guess she saw her chance with Jantzen and grabbed him. Since then, from all I hear, she's helped him in his affairs as much as she helped Elizabeth Jantzen."

"Any information turn up as to why Iris was so opposed to the marriage of Leland and Anne?" Mason asked.

"If you put two and two and two and two and two and two, etcetera, together, I think you could come up with a pretty reasonable answer to that question."

"How do you mean, Paul?"

"Well"—Drake took a deep breath—"from what I hear, Anne Kimbro has a pretty bad track record of getting involved with men most likely to cause her grief. The earliest example was when she was still in her teens and headed for Mexico with a guitar player to get married. They didn't; they turned back at the border, and she came home. Later, she told friends that by the time she and the guitar player reached the border, they'd run out of things to talk about and wondered what they'd find to say to one another for the rest of their lives if they got married. That was the easiest experience she had."

Drake took a sip of coffee. "Then there was a phony count in Paris she was going to marry, a TV soap-opera actor here in Hollywood, a young doctor who hadn't set up his first practice yet, a screenwriter who neglected to tell her he still wasn't divorced until after she'd told people they were to be married. And a couple of others. Some of them had to be bought off by the Jantzens. The prevailing opinion is that most of these characters hoped to cash in when she came into her inheritance. To Iris, I guess John Leland looked like just the latest in a long line of losers, hoping to hit the jackpot through marriage to Anne."

Mason shook his head. "None of that sounds like the proper young lady she appears to be today. It could have been that she was rebelling against the circumstances of her life."

"It happens, sure," Drake agreed. "At any rate, apparently for the last year or so she quieted down. She still lives the good life that money can buy, but my sources say Iris, and maybe Jantzen, convinced her that if she wasn't careful, sooner or later she'd create a scandal and revive the earlier scandal of her mother's murder. It's said that Iris, in particular, used a considerable amount of the Questall fortune to buy family respectability through donations to museums and the latest charity, even though none of them denied themselves whatever they wanted. The difference is they did it, they do it, as much as possible out of public view."

"So"—Mason smiled—"you're saying whatever their vices, and there are likely to be some we don't know about, they use their fortune to conceal them rather than flaunt them."

Drake nodded. "That's the way I see it, yes."

Mason rubbed the back of his hand against the bottom of his chin. "That leaves us with a lot we still have to find out if Phillips indicts Leland. For now, though, you did a good job, Paul."

Mason told Drake about his visit to Leland's real estate office, and shook his head. "Leland's secretary, Ginny Rollins, really wants to help him. However, unless Ray Dallas gets an entirely different story from her than I got, she's not going to be able to do Leland much good, I'm afraid."

As they finished their lunch, Drake, looking past Mason, said softly, "Here comes a real beauty. She's caught the eye of every man in the room, and unless I miss my guess, she's looking for you, Perry."

Mason half turned in his chair and saw Anne Kimbro approaching. He stood up quickly, and so did Drake, as she extended her hand to Mason.

"I'm sure I'm intruding, Mr. Mason. I'm sorry, but it's very important that I talk with you. When I went to your office, your secretary told me you were lunching here. She thought I might catch you before you left. I hope you don't mind."

"Not at all, Anne," Mason said. He introduced her to Drake.

"Actually, your timing was just right," Drake assured her. "I was ready to leave. It was nice meeting you. See you later, Perry."

Drake left.

Mason pulled out a chair for Anne Kimbro. "Would you like some lunch, coffee, or a drink, perhaps?"

"No thank you, Mr. Mason. What I would like, I guess, is a sympathetic hearing."

Mason nodded.

She said, "The police came to my house last night to question me. Lieutenant Dallas and another detective. They asked me a lot of questions, about John, how we met, why Iris was opposed to our marriage." She looked down at the tabletop. "I'm afraid that what I was able to tell them didn't help him much." She looked up. "But the truth is, I didn't, I don't, have anything to tell that would help him. What bothers me most is that I just don't know what I feel about John Leland anymore. My mind is in such turmoil."

"Why don't you tell me about it," Mason suggested quietly.

"Can you possibly understand what it's like to love someone, to trust them, to think you know them so well—and then to find out that they're a completely different person? A stranger, really, that you've never known, as it turns out. That's how I feel about John."

Mason said, "I think your feelings are understandable under the circumstances."

She looked at him searchingly. "Do you? You don't think I'm being unfair to him? That *I* may be wrong?"

"Before I try to answer that question, I have to ask you a question."

She nodded. "Yes. All right."

"Do you feel the way you do now about him because he didn't tell you who he really was? Or is it because he's a suspect in your stepmother's murder?"

She thought for a moment before she answered, "If I'm going to be completely honest, I'd have to say it's because he didn't tell me who he really was."

Mason smiled. "I thought that was what you'd say."

"Don't you see?" she said. "It's as if he didn't trust me enough to confide in me. I think I could have dealt with the facts if he had just told me. How can I think he didn't tell me because he didn't trust me?"

"Perhaps," Mason suggested, "it was because he didn't trust himself enough, because he felt he had to wait until the right moment came before he could tell you. Would that be easier for you to accept?"

"Maybe," she said. But she appeared doubtful.

Mason looked at her intently. "I'm not trying to put

thoughts into your head. You must follow your own feelings. You asked if I thought you were being unfair to him. My answer would be that you must make up your own mind about that. I trust you enough to believe that's what you'll do, because whatever decision you make, you're going to have to live with it for the rest of your life. And so is he."

"You're right, of course." She smiled suddenly. "You *have* given me a sympathetic hearing, and some good advice. Now, I have to ask for more help from you. And this is the real reason why it was important to me to find you as soon as possible."

Mason waited.

She said, "It's my stepfather, Mr. Mason. He's really not well. I'm worried for him. He's been, well, almost out of control with rage ever since he learned of Iris's murder. He's convinced that John killed her. He doesn't understand why the police haven't locked John up, and he doesn't understand why a famous, respected attorney like you would defend John. He's been phoning everybody he knows to get them to put pressure on the authorities to arrest John. And believe me, Mr. Mason, he knows some pretty important people."

Mason said, "Yes, I do know. The zealous activities of the D.A. and the police in this case have already made me aware of that fact." Mason paused before he added, "And I would assume that you have borne a good bit of the brunt of his rage."

She answered simply, "Yes." Then she said, "But as difficult as that is to contend with, it's not my real concern. My fear is that his overwrought state of mind will bring on another stroke, and that this time it will be fatal. That's why I thought perhaps you would help me."

"Gladly. But what can I do?"

She leaned forward. "Would you see my stepfather, talk to him, explain the case to him? I think it would help calm him down."

Mason answered quickly, "Certainly. I'll be glad to talk to him. When do you want me to do it?"

"Now," she said.

7

The house in Beverly Hills, unlike the one in Coldwater Canyon, looked as if it had been crafted by master carpenters who had spared no care or expense to make it a showcase in this community of showcase houses. Acres of lawn and garden surrounded the house, and a high wall surrounded the grounds. In back were a swimming pool and tennis courts, a guest house, and a multiple-car garage.

Mason, who had followed Anne Kimbro to Beverly Hills in his own car, joined her at the front entrance to the house. The door was opened by a butler in a white jacket. Behind the butler one of the doors on the far side of the wide hall opened, and Neal Granin came out and hurried toward Mason and Anne.

Granin shook hands with Mason. "Any new developments in the case?"

"Not yet," Mason said, "but I'm hoping."

Granin said, "Anyway, I'm still glad John has you for a lawyer."

"I take it then that you still don't think John Leland could be guilty?"

"No way. Not if I'm any judge of character."

Anne said softly, "I wish I could be as sure."

Granin put his arm around her shoulder protectively as he said to Mason, "Of course, I want whoever killed my sister to be convicted. It's just that I want the police to get the right person."

"We agree on that," Mason said.

"If there's anything I can do to help," Granin said, "you only have to ask."

Mason nodded. "I may want to talk to you again, at a later time."

Anne took a deep breath and said, "Come on, Mr. Mason, let's go see Daddy Jantzen."

Mason and Granin followed her across the hall and into the library.

Benjamin Jantzen sat in a mechanized wheelchair in front of a ceiling-high bookcase filled with leatherbound volumes.

The old man's eyes were closed, and for the split second before he opened his eyes, Mason thought fleetingly that the figure in the wheelchair could have been mistaken for an embalmed corpse. The gaunt face had a waxy sheen. The eyes were sunken hollows. The dark suit Jantzen wore was too large for his wasted frame. His left arm lay across his lap, the hand curled inward so the fingers almost touched his left wrist.

Anne hurried across the room and kissed the old man on the cheek. She turned and motioned Mason forward, saying, "This is Mr. Perry Mason. I told you I was going to ask him to come talk to you about John Leland."

Mason said, "Nice to meet you, sir."

Jantzen fixed his eyes on Mason, then made a motion of dismissal with his right hand toward Anne and Neal Granin.

His words, when he spoke, were as a result of his strokes hesitant, the sentences barely formed. "Leave us alone to talk," he told Anne.

Anne frowned, but she and Granin left the room, closing the door behind them.

Jantzen made another motion, toward the chair next to him. Mason sat. The old man worked a switch on the side of the wheelchair with his right hand, and the wheelchair half turned and stopped, facing Mason.

Jantzen's eyes closed and opened and he spoke.

"He killed her. Iris. The police know it!"

Mason said quietly, "John Leland is entitled to due process of law, Mr. Jantzen. No one *knows* that he killed your wife. Only evidence and a trial can determine that fact."

The old man shook his head slowly.

"He killed her. He comes from bad blood. He admitted it. He's his father's son."

"If he didn't do it," Mason said patiently, "would you still want to see him convicted?"

Jantzen didn't answer.

Mason leaned forward. "Let me ask you, why are you so certain he killed Iris? What was his motive?"

"Iris knew what he was up to."

"And what was that?"

"To trick Anne."

"Trick her how?" Mason asked.

"He wanted her money. Iris knew that. That's why she didn't want Anne to marry him."

Mason frowned. "What money?"

"He knew. In a few months Anne inherits . . . everything. She will be very rich. So would he be if she married him."

"Did Iris ever confront him, tell him that was what she suspected?"

The old man rocked back and forth in his wheelchair.

"That would have been the reason why she went to that house that afternoon."

"Do you know that for a fact?" Mason asked sternly. "Did Iris tell you she was going to see him for that reason?"

Jantzen didn't answer.

Mason said, "Then there's no proof that's what happened."

"I know that's what happened." Jantzen put his hand up to the left side of his chest. "I know. Here in my heart."

The old man swung his wheelchair around again and closed his eyes. This time he didn't open them again.

Mason sat waiting. Then he leaned close to make sure Jantzen was still breathing. Mason saw that the old man was all right, and he got up and went out.

Anne was waiting for him in the hall.

"Were you able to talk to him?" she asked anxiously.

Mason shrugged. "I talked, but he didn't want to hear what I had to say."

Anne smiled sadly. "I'm sorry, Mr. Mason. I thought maybe you'd be able to make him understand why the police haven't arrested John yet, why you're trying to defend him."

"I think he understands that part of it, all right. He

knows how the law works. He wasn't rude to me personally. The problem is that in his own mind he's already
put John Leland on trial and found him guilty; the verdict
of a one-man jury. I learned a long time ago that it does
no good to try to argue with a closed mind."

Anne sighed. "Well . . . thank you again, Mr. Mason.
It was kind of you to take the time to talk to him, even
if it did little good."

She had a large manila envelope in her hands, which
she handed to Mason. She explained the envelope contained a collection of copies of anonymous threatening
letters sent to Iris Jantzen and, earlier, to Benjamin
Jantzen. She said she had given copies to Lieutenant Dallas, but he had seemed to believe they were the work of
a crank. She had wanted Mason to see them. He took the
envelope.

She walked him to the door, and he went out to his
car. As he headed away from the house through the gates
in the high wall surrounding the Jantzen property, his
car phone buzzed.

Drake said, "Perry, I'm at the courthouse. I just got a
tip. Phillips is ready to move with an indictment of Leland. They're preparing to pick him up now."

"Thanks, Paul."

Mason quickly dialed Leland's office.

Leland answered.

"This is Perry Mason, John. I'm on my way to your
office. I want you to stay there until I arrive. It shouldn't
be more than a matter of minutes."

Mason drove fast.

He hadn't wanted to alert Leland that the police were
on the way. There was always the chance that Leland
might panic and run again, guilty or not.

Fifteen minutes later, when Mason parked in front of

Leland's office in Culver City, he was relieved to see there were no police cars on the street.

Leland was waiting in the doorway to his office.

Mason took him by the arm and led him inside as Leland asked anxiously, "What is it, Mr. Mason? What's going on?"

Mason said, "It's all right, John. I want you to stay calm. The police are on their way here now to arrest you."

"Oh, my God!"

Leland's secretary, Ginny Rollins, was watching them wide-eyed.

"Listen to me," Mason said forcefully. "We always knew this was a possibility. This isn't the end of the world. What will happen now is that we'll appear before a judge, plead not guilty, and have you freed on bail. The next step, after a time, will be a preliminary hearing before a second judge, at which time I expect to convince the court to drop the charges."

Mason was silent for a moment before he asked gently, "That doesn't sound too terrible, does it?"

"I guess . . . not," Leland said tentatively.

Mason's manner became brisk. "Now, when the police get here, I want you to remain calm. I'll be with you throughout the proceedings. Okay?"

Leland nodded.

Mason had been glancing out the window from time to time as he talked. He said now, "Here they come."

Lieutenant Ray Dallas entered the office first, followed by D.A. Carter Phillips, and two homicide detectives, McKeevy and another plainclothesman Mason knew only by sight.

Phillips appeared disappointed when he saw Mason waiting with Leland.

The D.A. came and stood in front of Leland, holding up a document.

Phillips said officiously, "John Leland, I have a warrant for your arrest for the murder of Iris Jantzen."

Mason held out a hand. "May I see that, please, Mr. Phillips?"

Phillips handed over the warrant.

Mason scanned the paper, noted the judge's signature, and gave it back to Phillips.

Mason said, his voice as formal as the D.A.'s had been, "As John Leland's attorney, I hearby notify you that I will surrender Mr. Leland to the court forthwith. I request that I be allowed to drive Mr. Leland to the courthouse."

Phillips hesitated, then turned toward Lieutenant Dallas.

Dallas said, "I see no problem with Mr. Mason's request. We'll follow them in."

Phillips still hesitated briefly before he finally shrugged, turned, and started back out the door.

Mason motioned to Leland, who followed Phillips, the two detectives directly behind Leland. Mason had waited so he could have a word with Dallas as they went out together.

"What prompted Phillips to act now, Ray?" Mason asked.

Dallas said softly, "Remember the missing gardener's glove? The left-handed glove we couldn't find at the house the night of the murder?"

"What about it?"

"The forensic guys discovered it when they were going over the murder scene again this afternoon. The glove had been stuffed into a crevice in the lower part of the chimney of the fireplace in the sunroom. The glove had bloodstains on it. Finding the glove, along with everything else D.A. Phillips thinks he has against Leland, decided him to move to indict."

Dallas glanced sideways at Mason. "Remember, Counselor, I warned you we'd find the glove."

Mason said nothing. As he turned to close the office door behind him, he saw Ginny Rollins sitting at her desk, weeping openly.

8

The morning newspapers and TV news shows all had lead stories on the arrest of John Leland the day before.

Drake sat in the big leather client's chair in front of Mason's desk reading one of the newspapers while Mason emptied out his briefcase of the papers he'd brought into the office with him that morning. He put the manila envelope containing the anonymous threatening letters Anne Kimbro had given him into the desk drawer. He'd read the letters and guessed they might be the work of Bernard Newcombe, who had lost his lawsuits against Questall Pharmaceuticals.

"So, how did Leland hold up at the indictment proceedings?" Drake asked.

"Better than I expected," Mason said. "I think his worst moment was when Phillips asked for bail of two-hundred-fifty-thousand dollars. Leland didn't realize then that I could ask for a lower amount and the judge would grant it. Fifty thousand, as it turned out, on Leland's signature bond. Despite the fact that Leland disappeared once, the judge took into consideration Leland's business assets and ties to the community."

Mason looked bemused as he went on to say, "I don't think Leland was concerned about not being able to raise bail for the larger amount; it was that what he faced seemed less serious if he was freed for the lower amount rather than the larger one. I guess our minds are conditioned to react that way."

Drake folded up the newspaper and placed it on the desk. "If the news accounts are right, it looks like Phillips has a strong case against our client."

Della Street tapped on the door and came into the office in time to hear Drake's last remark.

She said quickly, "Good morning, Chief. Paul, I didn't know you were here."

"Come on in, Della," Mason said. "Paul's just explaining to me how the D.A.'s going to make me look silly in court when I try to defend Leland."

Drake raised a hand. "Hold on now, Perry! I didn't finish what I had to say, which is, I'd like to know what you have up your sleeve."

Mason looked up from the papers he was sorting out on his desk. "There's nothing up my sleeve, Paul. What I have is a hunch the District Attorney's Office is under pressure to get into court with this case before they're fully prepared—something they may regret later. That's why I asked for an early preliminary hearing. When the judge set the hearing for next week, I was surprised Phillips eagerly agreed."

"You don't think they have enough on Leland to convince the court he should go to trial?" Drake asked, the doubt in his voice clearly indicating his feelings.

Mason put his hands down on the desk and leaned forward. "Let me put it this way: There are an awful lot of unexamined possible motives and possible suspects involved in the murder of Iris Jantzen. How can the D.A. know about them if he doesn't even take the time to investigate them?"

"Which is where we come in, right?" Drake said. "I get it."

"You got it!" Mason grinned. "For instance, what about this guy who's been suing the company over the years? What about the threatening letters Iris received, presumably from him? But maybe not. I'd want to know."

"You mean Newcombe."

Mason nodded. "Him, yes. And what about the relationships between all these people who are so intertwined? What does anyone know about how Anne Kimbro got along with Iris, for example?"

Della interrupted, curious. "Do you mean you think Anne Kimbro could have killed Iris?"

"I mean," Mason said, "I'd like to know how Anne felt about Iris. Here was a woman, Iris, who marries the man Anne's mother was married to—and neither the man, Jantzen, nor Iris have any connection to Anne except by the earlier marriage of Anne's mother. Did Anne resent Iris? Did she resent Jantzen marrying Iris? I'd like to know."

Mason paused and frowned. "Then there's the residue from the earlier murder of Elizabeth Jantzen. What about Edward Larner's brother, Joseph, who apparently believes he got cut out of money that should rightfully have been his? What do we know about him?"

Mason, out of habit, had begun pacing as he articulated his thoughts. "For that matter, what about the missing Edward Larner himself? Who knows where he is or, after twenty years, even what he might look like today?"

Della shook her head and looked at Drake, smiling. "Paul, it sounds to me like Perry's hinting you have some legwork to do."

Paul grinned and held up a sheet of paper on which he had been scribbling notes while Mason spoke. "I got the message loud and clear."

Mason stopped pacing and smiled. "I don't expect you to get answers to all the questions I've raised, Paul." He paused and said, "Just the important ones."

Paul jumped to his feet. "Let me out of here before you think of something else."

Mason said, "Actually, there is one more thing. When Phillips and Dallas were questioning John Leland, they asked him if on the day of Iris's murder he had seen any of the neighbors who live close to the house in Coldwater Canyon. Which would indicate that they mean to canvass the people in the area to see if any of them saw Leland."

Paul nodded. "And what you want is a similar canvass, to see if anyone else might have been in the vicinity that day. I'll put a couple of men on it."

After Paul had gone, Della said, "I have a question, Chief."

"Yes, Della?"

"I followed all the news accounts that have appeared today, and one of the things that seems weakest to me is the motive John Leland might have had for killing Iris. I gather from the news that D.A. Phillips is going to claim he killed Iris because she was opposed to the marriage of Leland and Anne. If I were deciding the case, that motive would sound awfully flimsy to me. Is that the best they can come up with?"

"Good point, Della," Mason said. "Actually, when I

spoke with the old man, Jantzen, he added weight to that possible motive. His theory is that Iris believed Leland knew that Anne was about to come into a large inheritance that he'd share, and, Jantzen theorizes, Iris confronted Leland with her suspicions that that was the real reason he wanted to marry Anne."

Della frowned. "Did Jantzen tell you he had any proof Iris actually accused Leland of this?"

"The old man never answered me directly on the point."

"And I suppose he's told the D.A. the same thing?"

"I would imagine so," Mason said. "But we do have one factor operating to our advantage as far as Jantzen and his theory are concerned."

"What's that?"

Mason said, "Phillips is never going to be able to get Jantzen into court to testify. Jantzen's in no condition to appear in a courtroom. I doubt that any doctor would permit it."

Mason glanced at his watch. "I'm going to be out of the office for a while. I've arranged to meet John Leland at the house where Iris was murdered. I want to take him through his actions, step by step, that day from the time he arrived at the house and found her body up until the police got there. If I decide to put Leland on the stand, I don't want to take any chances that Phillips will trip him up on those crucial minutes while he was there alone. And I want to go through it all with Leland while it should still be fresh in his mind."

9

Mason said, "Now you arrived here at the front door—show me everything you did from this point until the first police officers got here."

Leland nodded. "I had seen the car parked there." He pointed to the driveway.

"Iris's car?"

"Anne's family has several cars. They use them interchangeably. I did recognize that the car parked here that day was usually driven by Iris, so, yes, it did occur to me that Iris was in the house. Still, I couldn't imagine why she would be. I'd never encountered her here before."

Mason said, "In any event you believed someone was in the house?"

"Yes. I knocked on the front door. I tried to open it with the key Anne gave me. When the door wouldn't budge, I knew it had been secured by the deadbolt lock inside."

Leland walked away from the door around the side of the house. Mason followed. Police had strung around the house a yellow tape with the warning CRIME SCENE. DO NOT ENTER.

At the door to the glassed-in sunroom at the side of the house in back, Leland said, "I tried this door, and it was locked. I didn't have a key. I looked into the room, and that's when I saw the body."

Mason said, "Show me exactly where you stood when you looked into the sunroom."

Leland took a step and pointed.

Mason moved to the spot. He was able to see inside where the chalk outline left behind by the forensic team indicated the place the body had been found.

"As I told you before," Leland went on, "when I saw the body, I thought it might be Anne. I put my fist through the glass in the door near the doorknob, stuck my hand inside, unlocked the door, opened it, and went in."

The section where the glass had been broken in the door was boarded over with a strip of wood.

Earlier Mason had informed Ray Dallas that he wanted to visit the house with Leland. Dallas had no objection, since all the evidence had been removed.

"Let's go in now," Mason said.

The two men walked back to the front of the house, Leland opened the door with his key, and they went down the long hall to the sunroom.

Mason went over to the door Leland said he had entered through on the day of the murder. He stood in front of the door. "You entered here, right?"

"Yes." Leland crossed to the chalk marks. "And I walked over here and looked at—at the body. And I saw it wasn't Anne."

"Did you touch the body?"

"I—" Leland hesitated. "I don't know, for sure. As well as I can recall, once I knew it wasn't Anne lying there, I realized my hand was bleeding, and I took out my handkerchief and wrapped it around my hand. And then I went to the phone and called the police."

"Hold on," Mason interrupted. "Are you saying you went directly to the phone and called? Didn't you tell me the day I first talked to you here that you considered simply leaving, and then, after you thought it over, you decided you had no choice but to notify the police?"

"Yes."

"The point is," Mason said firmly, "if you did that, then you didn't go directly to the phone after you'd seen Iris's body, as you're telling me now."

"There was that brief period in between," Leland admitted. "But I can't see how that could have any significance."

Mason pointed a finger. "I'll tell you how it could have some possible significance. There will be an exact-time record when your call was received by the police. D.A. Phillips will have that record. If you take the witness stand and he questions you as I just have and he happens to find a witness who can testify as to the time you were seen arriving at the house, he'll work backward in time. There must not be any gaps in time that you don't account for. Understand? Even though it may not have any real bearing on the case, he can use it to try to confuse you and make you look evasive."

"I get it."

"Good. Now after you phoned the police, what did you do?"

"I tried to phone Anne. But there was no answer."

Mason frowned. "Doesn't she live with the rest of the family in the house in Beverly Hills? Didn't anyone answer the phone?"

"She lives there, yes," Leland said. "But she has a private line of her own. I called her on that line. When she didn't answer, I didn't call any of the other phone numbers at the house. I didn't want to talk to anyone else there."

"What did you do next?"

Leland shrugged. "Nothing, really. I paced back and forth for maybe five minutes, and then Anne phoned me here. I told her what had happened. We agreed I should have a lawyer. We ended the call, I paced up and down some more, and she phoned back and said you were coming to represent me. The next thing, the police were here."

"How did they get into the house?"

"I heard the sound of the siren, and I went to the front door and opened it."

"Opened the deadbolt lock?" Mason asked.

"Yes. Why?"

"Because if there had been any fingerprints on that lock, and there should have been if the lock was on when you got here, your prints would have blurred or even erased them."

"Oh, Lord, I see," Leland said miserably, shaking his head. "I never thought of that at the time. I guess if they took fingerprints off the lock, they were mine."

Mason said, "They took prints off that lock. You can count on it."

Before Mason could say anything else, there was the sound of a car driving up outside.

Mason glanced away and then back at Leland. "What happened when the police came?"

"I told them what had happened. How I had come here and found Iris dead. One of the policemen went to the phone right away. The other one tried to ask me questions. I told him I wouldn't answer any questions until you were present. I asked them if I could sit down. They said I could. Then the other policeman, Lieutenant Dallas and two other men, came. They tried to ask me questions. I told them what I had already told the first policeman; that I wouldn't talk to them until you were here."

There was the sound of the front door opening and closing and footsteps coming along the hall.

Mason had moved over to the fireplace. He asked hurriedly, "Did you come anywhere near this fireplace? Did you happen to touch it? Any part of it?"

Leland said, "No."

Anne Kimbro walked into the sunroom.

"Anne!" Mason said, turning toward her. "I hope finding us here didn't startle you."

"No. I saw your cars outside," she said. "Is it all right for me to have come in?"

Mason smiled. "It's your house. I'm afraid we're the intruders. There were just a few things I wanted to talk over with John here at the house."

"I understand, Mr. Mason. Besides, I don't think of this as my house anymore. I think of it now as belonging to, well, I suppose, to the police, the authorities, whatever, until all of this is resolved, over with."

Mason said, "At any rate, we've finished our business here."

For the first time since she'd entered the sunroom, Anne looked directly at John Leland.

Leland flushed and said quietly, "Hello, Anne."

For a moment she didn't speak. Finally, she said, "Hello, John," and turned away.

Leland flushed again and said stiffly, "Is there anything else, Mr. Mason?"

Mason's answer was quite gentle. "No, John, not for now. I'll be talking to you again soon. Try not to worry any more than you can help. Most of what has to be done from here on is my job."

Leland nodded wordlessly. He hesitated, looking at Anne. She had her head turned away from him. He walked out of the room, and there was the sound of his footsteps receding in the hall, the sound of the front door closing, and, in a little while, the sound of his car starting up and driving away.

Mason had been silently watching Anne. She didn't turn her head until Leland had driven off.

Mason took a check from his pocket and handed it to Anne Kimbro. "John paid me a retainer, Anne. I'm returning the money you paid me."

Anne took the check.

Mason said, "I guess I'll be going, too."

Anne put out a hand. "Wait just a minute, please. There's something I want to get. I'll leave with you. Suddenly, I don't want to be here alone."

She went to the small table where the telephone sat, reached under the table, and held out a large book.

"A photograph album," she said. "I remembered that I'd brought it here a while back and had forgotten to take it home again. When I thought of it, I was afraid maybe the police had taken it away."

She ran her hand over the front of the album. "It was my mother's. I've had it since I was a little girl. Over the years I've added my own photographs to it. That way I always felt it was something we shared, both our memories preserved together." She looked up. "Have you ever seen a picture of my mother?"

"No," Mason said. "But I'd like to."

Anne came over and stood close to him and opened the album.

On the first page was a color photograph of a beautiful young woman. Her face looked serene, her hair blond, combed back from her face, her eyes a startling sea green, the color of Anne's eyes.

"She was lovely," Mason said.

"This was the last photograph taken of her, only a few days before . . . before she died. It's such a beautiful picture of her that I moved it to the first page of the album."

Mason continued to look at the photograph. Before now, when he read, or thought about, the murder of Elizabeth Jantzen, he had never visualized her as so youthful-looking, so vital, at the time of her death. It came as a small shock to him that when she died, she hadn't been more than a few years older than Anne was now. The new knowledge made her long-ago murder seem more immediate—he felt it more personally than he had when reading the news accounts.

"Let me show you something," Anne said, riffling through the pages toward the back of the album with one hand, while with the other hand she marked a place in the front of the album.

"See here," she said. "Here she is when she was a baby. And here"—she flipped the pages—"I am. And here, when she was a little girl, and here, me at about the same age."

She turned the pages back and forth through the album, showing first photographs of her mother, then of herself.

"There's a remarkable resemblance between you and your mother," Mason said, meaning it.

Anne's smile, in return, was radiant. "You couldn't have paid me a nicer compliment."

She turned the pages toward the back of the album, showing him later pictures of herself. "Here I am in the gawky stage, when I didn't look much like my mother, I'm afraid."

Mason noticed that after a few more pages, as the photographs showed Anne at a later age, in her early and late teens, there was always the same boy with her.

Curious, he asked, "Who's that with you?"

"Don't you recognize him? That's Neal Granin, Iris's younger brother."

She showed Mason more photographs of herself with Neal Granin—one showed her a teenager in a party frock, Neal dressed in a dark suit; another displayed her in her late teens, with Neal a young man by then, both posed in front of the Eiffel Tower in Paris.

She said, "From the time I was a little girl, after Iris married Daddy Jantzen and she and Neal came to live with us, he was my companion, my escort."

"Your big brother?"

She nodded. "In a way, yes. More like my confidant, I guess. I always felt I could tell him anything."

"How about Iris? How did you get along with her?"

Anne looked at Mason and raised an eyebrow. "I wonder why you asked me that question, as if I didn't know. Are you trying to uncover some family secrets?"

Mason said, "I'd rather you thought I was trying to get a clear idea of the person Iris was." He waited.

She repeated his question. "How did I get along with Iris? For openers, she was always kind to me, although I think other people found her cold and too aggressive, perhaps."

"Was she? With other people, I mean?"

"There are those who thought so, from what I gathered. Daddy Jantzen once explained to me that Iris hadn't had an easy life—trying to support herself and Neal—before she married him. He also told me that she was important to him, particularly because of his strokes, and to his business. Our business. I think that at the time he told me that he didn't want me to resent Iris because they'd married, that he wanted me to like her."

"And did you?" Mason asked.

"Yes."

"And you never felt she was usurping your own mother's place?"

"There wasn't any reason for me to feel that," Anne answered. "For one thing, I was never with either of them much when I was growing up. I was educated in schools abroad from the time I was out of grade school. During most of that time about the only person I saw connected with the family was Neal. He would come over to wherever I was, Paris, Switzerland, regularly to visit me. I always suspected they'd sent him over from time to time to keep an eye on me, to make sure I was all right."

"And Jantzen himself? What were your feelings about him?"

She frowned. "Looking back on the years I was growing up, I guess now I'd say that I thought of him as . . . distant would be the word. A lot of that feeling came from the fact that he was in a wheelchair, you know. So, he wasn't like other people. Later on, when I was old enough and was told the story about my mother and what happened to her, I think I pitied him. Much as I loved my mother, I felt sympathy for him. I would see him right in front of me and feel he was somewhere else, at least in his thoughts. When I would think about it, I always imagined he'd suffered a double loss. First, he lost her to another man—no matter that she had made the decision to stay with him and break off with the other man—and then there was the second loss, forever, when she was killed."

She looked around the sunroom wonderingly. "I've thought a lot about my mother over the years. About how she must have loved another man but felt she had to stop seeing him and then ended up dead for what she did. If she really loved Edward Larner, why didn't she just run off with him, whatever the consequences?"

"Have you ever thought she was trying to do what she thought was the right thing?" Mason asked gently.

"Yes. But so many people suffered as a result."

"That's the way it is sometimes," he told her. "People get themselves into situations innocently enough in the beginning, and when they try to get out without hurting anyone, it often ends up with everyone being hurt."

"I've tried to put myself in her place," Anne said. "That's one reason why I've been so attached to this house and wanted to complete it and live here. I wanted to see if that would help me understand better what she went through and what happened to her. It sounds, well, maybe a bit mystical, but I thought perhaps that's why she left the house to me, separate from the rest of the estate."

She looked down at the open photograph album. "But now, ever since Iris, too, was murdered here, I almost believe the house has a curse on it. One thing's for sure. I no longer ever want to live here."

She had reached the last few pages in the album. Mason could see that those pages were filled with photographs of Anne and John Leland. She made no comment on those pictures and closed the album.

She squared her shoulders and looked at Mason. "I don't think I even want to return here ever again."

10

Back in his office Mason was stopped by Gertie, the receptionist, as soon as he came through the door from the hall.

"That man over there"—Gertie nodded to the far side of the reception area—"has been waiting to see you. His name is Joseph Larner."

Mason nodded, crossed to where Larner was sitting, and stuck out his hand.

"Mr. Larner, you wanted to see me? I'm Perry Mason."

Larner got to his feet quickly, grabbed Mason's hand, and pumped it vigorously.

"It's a real pleasure to meet you, Mr. Mason. I've followed your cases in the papers and on TV for years. Never thought I'd have occasion to meet you." He held up one of the morning newspapers. "And now here you are, a crackerjack lawyer, representing my nephew, John. I'd sure like to talk to you, if you could spare me the time."

"Yes, all right, come on in."

Joseph Larner was a lanky man, gray-haired, with a face that looked weathered from time spent outdoors. He settled himself in any easy slouch into the chair across the desk from Mason.

"He didn't do it, you know," Larner said, wasting no time in making clear his intention for wanting to see Mason. "John Leland didn't kill that woman. I don't know what it is; it seems like the women in that family are a fatal lure for the men in my family. My brother, Edward, should have stayed away from Elizabeth, and John from Anne Kimbro. I told both of them the same thing twenty years apart."

"When did you tell John that?" Mason asked, curious.

"As soon as he found out who Anne really was. By then it was too late; he was already in love with her, just as his father had been in love with her mother. They both, Edward and John, thought that somehow they could make things turn out right in both instances."

Mason tried to make his next question sound offhand. "Did you ever try to do anything to break up the relationship between John and Anne?"

"Do anything? You mean besides try to talk to him?"

"Or talk to anyone else?"

"Why would I do that?"

"Well, if anyone in Anne's family knew who John really was, before he revealed it, it might have been a way of ending the relationship right there," Mason suggested. "For instance, if someone told Iris—"

Larner sat upright in the chair suddenly. "Hold on, Mr. Mason! Are you saying I might have talked to that woman?"

Mason said soothingly, "Take it easy, Mr. Larner. I'm John's lawyer. We're going into court soon on a murder charge. I have to know before then if somehow the D.A. has found out you, or somebody else, might have told Iris. If so, the D.A. puts that person on the stand and forces that person to testify to the fact. Then the D.A. claims that's why Iris sought John out the day of the murder. I'm caught by surprise, and the D.A. has a pretty solid motive for John having killed her."

Larner settled back into the chair. "I see what you're driving at now, Mr. Mason. But I guarantee you, I won't be the person he puts on the stand."

"You do understand why I had to ask you the question?"

"I do. No offense taken. Anything you ask that'll help John I'll answer."

"Fine," Mason said. "Let's talk about your brother, Edward, and the earlier murder of Elizabeth."

Larner spread his hands. "What would you like me to tell you?"

"I believe you were the one who discovered Elizabeth's body in the house in Coldwater Canyon, isn't that correct?"

"Yes, sir, I did."

"Did you have any idea where Edward might have disappeared to? Someplace nobody else but you would have known about?"

Larner looked at Mason levelly. "At the time, the police asked me the same question."

Mason half smiled. "Never mind what the police asked you then. Or what you answered them. I'm asking you now."

Larner grinned. "I told the police I didn't know of any place."

"But you did know," Mason said softly.

Larner nodded. "Yeah, I did. A cabin in the Sierra Mountains. Edward and I used to go fishing up there when we were young men."

"You looked for him there?"

"I did."

"And?"

Larner shook his head. Mason thought he looked as if he wanted to say something else.

"What is it?" Mason asked. "There's more."

Larner said reluctantly, "You're right. He wasn't there. But it looked like he might have been, recently, before I got there. I couldn't be sure."

Mason frowned. "What would you have done if you'd found him?"

"I'd have gotten him to turn himself in."

"And have seen him go to prison, probably for life."

"Oh, I don't think that would have happened, Mr. Mason," Larner said.

"No? Why not?"

Larner sat forward in the chair. "Because they'd have found him not guilty by reason of temporary insanity. The way that man was obsessed by Elizabeth, building them a house and all, he'd just have had to have gone clear out of his mind when she told him it was over with him—and that's when and why he killed her."

Mason had a sudden thought. "Did you ever try to find him in the years since then?"

"I sure have. At one point, and for a while, I started getting money orders in the mail from different parts of the country. No name, no address. I took it to be money meant for John. I gave it to John's aunt, Janine, who was taking care of him. But she wouldn't have anything to do with the money, and told the police about the money orders. I guess Edward caught on to what was happening, and he stopped sending the money. And all that time I was trying to find him."

"How did you go about trying to find him?" Mason asked.

"I'd hire private detectives to look for him. Every time a money order would arrive from whatever city, I'd hire a private detective there to look for him."

"So," Mason said, "you have no idea where he might be now?"

"No, sir."

"Did you ever think perhaps he might be somewhere around here, nearby, and nobody knows it?"

Larner appeared puzzled. Then he said slowly, "You don't think—he could have come back after all these years—could have anything to do with—with the murder of Iris? You don't think that, do you?"

"Let me ask you a question, Mr. Larner." Mason drummed on his desk softly with the tips of his fingers. "If you were working out an equation, wouldn't the logical way to go about it be to consider all the imponderables so you'd arrive at the correct result?"

"Yes, sir," Larner said. "I can see that."

"Okay. The same thing applies to working out the solution to a murder. Which is what we're trying to do now."

Larner said, "I can follow what you're saying. But the problem with thinking Edward would come back here and kill Iris is, Why would he do that and have his own son be accused of the crime?"

"Ah, but if John got to the house after Iris was murdered, as John says he did, how could anyone have anticipated that he would be there and be charged with the crime?"

Larner nodded. "You're right about that part of it, all right."

Mason said sharply, "If you knew where Edward was right now, would you tell me? Would you tell the police?"

Larner's head jerked upright. "Sure I would! I've already told you it's important enough to me that I've been looking for him for years."

Mason appeared thoughtful. "That's right; it would be important to you to find Edward, wouldn't it? As I recall, you have a considerable amount of money coming to you that's been held up ever since Elizabeth was murdered and Edward disappeared."

"You've done some homework, Mr. Mason," Larner said, respect in his voice.

Mason nodded. "Also, as I recall, one of the reasons the money has never come to you through court action is because the matter has been contested by Benjamin Jantzen. And Iris Jantzen."

Larner smiled ruefully. "Now, we're back to that business of working out the equation, aren't we, Mr. Mason? Only this time *I'm* one of the imponderables."

"Aside from your concern for John, which I believe is sincere," Mason said, "wasn't one of the reasons you came to see me today to find out if you were—in the terms we've been using—one of the imponderables in the case?"

"By God," Larner said, grinning and shaking his head, "like I said when I first came in here today, you're a crackerjack lawyer."

11

Gertie said over the intercom, "Paul Drake's calling on line four."

"Got it, Gertie."

Mason picked up the phone. "Yes, Paul?"

"Perry, I think I may have something for you."

Mason swung around in his big swivel chair and propped his feet on the bottom desk drawer. "Let's hear it."

"I got a tip from a guy who's retired from the LAPD. He remembered something out of the past about Iris Jantzen. An investigation that went nowhere. He didn't work on the investigation himself, but he remembered a detective who did. The case was suspected blackmail by Iris. The case was never proven, but my contact was trying to do me a favor, and he thought we might want to look into it."

"It's worth a follow-up, all right. You never know where a lead will take you."

"I thought you'd say that," Drake said. "I tracked down the detective who was on the investigation and who is willing to talk—but it has to be with you, alone, and off the record. Those were the conditions."

"No problem, Paul. When can I see him?"

"How soon can you be in beautiful downtown Hollywood? The meeting place is a bar called Rosita's, a couple of blocks off Hollywood and Vine." Drake gave him the address.

"I can leave now," Mason said.

"Good. Incidentally, the detective's not a he; it's a she. Sergeant Shirley Culver. She's just going off duty. She'll wait with me in Rosita's until you get there."

"I'm on the way." Mason hung up the phone, buzzed Della Street to say he was leaving for the day, and went down and got his car out of the parking lot next to the Brill Building.

The sun was setting when he reached Rosita's and had to drive around the block a couple of times before he could find a place to park.

Paul and the policewoman were sitting at a table in the rear of the small bar. Paul stood, introduced Mason and Detective Culver, and left, telling Mason, "I'll be waiting outside in my car."

"Thanks, Paul."

Mason sat down. "I appreciate your talking to me, Sergeant."

Shirley Culver smiled. "I'm delighted to meet you, Mr. Mason, and to be in a position to do you a favor. Who knows? One day maybe I'll need a *favor* from you."

She was tall, nicely proportioned, auburn-haired, dark-eyed, with high cheekbones and a square chin. She looked to be in her late forties, and her manner was confident, relaxed.

A waiter came over to the table, and Mason ordered a drink for Sergeant Culver and one for himself.

"I thought this would be a good place for us to talk," she said. "I'm working undercover in the area now. There's a lot of felonious activity going on up and down the streets around here, but Rosita's is a safe oasis. I know them here, they know me."

She sat back in her chair. "Drake told me why you wanted to talk to me. You know the conditions."

Mason smiled. "Off the record. Agreed."

"The fact is," she said, "I don't know that what I have to tell you will do you much good. But, anyhow, Ed Broward asked me to talk to Drake and to you. Ed used to be my partner before he retired. I decided if Ed wanted me to tell you what I know, I'd do it."

The waiter brought the drinks.

Sergeant Culver took a sip of her drink. "What I'm going to tell you took place, oh, twenty-five years ago. I was just a rookie at the time, but I was assigned to this particular investigation involving Iris Jantzen, or, as she was known then, Iris Granin."

She took another sip of her drink. "There was this guy, his name was Harold Fadden, and he ran a nickle-and-dime mail-order business. She was his secretary. One day Harold Fadden comes in and tells the authorities his secretary, Iris, is trying to shake him down, blackmail him. She'd discovered that his mail-order business was a fraud, and, according to him, she tried to blackmail him by threatening to blow the whistle on him unless he paid her to keep quiet. Old Harold was desperate—otherwise he'd never have come in, because he admitted he was guilty of fraud. But he'd decided it would be better for him to tell the police than to keep on *and* still have to pay her off. And he wanted to nail her."

She shook her head. "Well, we did our best to trap her. Harold was fitted out with a wire, tried to get her to incriminate herself, but it didn't work. She must have sensed a trap. She never did or said anything to give herself away. So it was only his word, and we never had a case against her. Of course, we all believed Harold was telling the truth. After all, he was convicted and sent to prison for what he had revealed, and she walked away."

Mason nodded. "Interesting. And what became of Harold Fadden?"

"That's really why Ed Broward wanted me to talk to you."

She took a sip of her drink and put the glass down. "As I said, all of this was a long time ago. I would have forgotten all about it, except when Iris Granin married that Jantzen fellow, I saw it in the papers and remembered the Fadden case. Then I forgot all about her until she was murdered. When that story broke, Ed Broward called me, and we talked. It made us both think of Harold Fadden. Ed did a check on Fadden. You know what he found out? While Harold Fadden was in jail on the fraud charge, he and another inmate got into a fight, and Fadden killed the man. That got Fadden a long term in the pen. You can probably guess why Ed and I decided I should talk to you."

She looked at Mason and waited.

"Fadden got out recently, right?"

She nodded. "One month ago. On my own, I tried to find out what had become of him. What I discovered is that he's vanished. There's no trace of where he went."

She paused before she said, "You understand I'm not

trying to arrive at any conclusion about where he is or what he might have done since he was released?"

Mason said, "I understand perfectly. Nevertheless, I'm glad you told me about this. It can't hurt to see if we can locate him. Even if nothing comes of any of this, it's worth the effort of seeing what we can find out."

"I would think so," she said. "The Fadden case was one of those curious incidents buried beneath the surface of Iris's life that might have been passed over because it never became known publicly. And there may be no connection at all with her murder."

"Still, you never know," Mason said. "Thanks again for the information."

"You're welcome to whatever you can do with it." She smiled at him. "But I think we both know the D.A. wouldn't exactly recommend me for a citation for talking to you."

She stood, Mason paid the check, and they walked out of the bar.

Mason shook hands with her. "Sergeant, if you ever need that favor you mentioned, call me."

He watched her walk away, a bulky handbag—which he speculated probably carried her police revolver—slung over her shoulder.

Drake, waiting in his car parked near the bar, opened the door, and Mason slid inside to talk before he went to his own car. He told Drake the story Shirley Culver had told him and added, "I think you should assign a couple of men to see if they can pick up Fadden's trail."

"I'll get right on it," Drake said. "Funny, the things that turn up in a person's background."

"That's the way it is," Mason said. "Murder has a way of bringing out the worst in people."

12

Late Sunday afternoon Perry Mason was in his apartment when Lieutenant Ray Dallas telephoned.

Mason pushed aside the documents he'd been reading that had been supplied by D.A. Phillips. The documents contained the details of the murder charge against John Leland that would be the basis of the prosecution's case in the preliminary hearing on Tuesday.

On the phone Dallas said, "Perry, I just received a call from headquarters that there's a report of a bad fire at the house where Iris Jantzen was murdered in the canyon. I don't have any other information on the fire. I figured you'd want to know. I'm leaving to go out there now."

"Thanks, Ray. I'd better take a look myself."

"I thought you might want to," Dallas said, and hung up.

Fifty-five minutes later Mason turned his car into the blacktop driveway leading through the trees and foliage to Anne Kimbro's house in Coldwater Canyon. A dense pall of smoke hung over the area, obscuring the sky. A line of fire engines, pumpers, emergency vehicles, an ambulance, two chiefs' cars, and a couple of unmarked vehicles were parked at the side of the roadway.

Mason reached the clearing beyond the trees and parked.

The fire had leveled the house to the ground. A dozen firemen in rubber coats, helmets, and boots were pouring water and foam on the smoldering debris, sending waves of dark smoke drifting out across the canyon.

Mason spotted Ray Dallas standing at the edge of the clearing and hurried to join him.

Mason said, "Looks like a bad one, Ray. Any idea of how the fire started?"

Dallas turned. "I spoke to a fire marshal who was one of the first ones on the scene. He says that from the intensity of the heat when he first got here, he'd suspect that it might be an arson job."

"No sign of any fatalities, are there?" Mason asked.

"Not yet. But so far they haven't had a chance to search through the ruins. The reason we were notified so quickly at headquarters is because somebody at the LAFD remembered there'd been a recent murder here. They thought we should be told about the fire."

"Does Anne Kimbro know yet?"

"I called her from here on the car phone," Dallas said. "She seemed composed enough at hearing the news. She said she'd be here."

One of the firemen walked over to Mason and Dallas. Dallas introduced him to Mason as battalion chief Judson Stacy.

Stacy, whose face was streaked with soot, said, "Lucky we didn't have one of those Santa Ana winds blowing through here today. Could have turned the whole canyon into a furnace."

Dallas said, "One of the marshals I spoke to said it could have been the work of an arsonist."

Stacy pushed his helmet back on his head. "I hear the house had been vacant for a while. That would increase the odds the fire wasn't accidental. You'd figure maybe some firebug or vandal torched it. In addition, somebody said there'd been a murder here not too long ago. Sure, the marshals would have suspicions. So do I. I'd have some questions to ask the owner, too."

"The owner will be along soon," Dallas said. "I phoned and told her about the fire."

"Good," Stacy said, and walked away.

Dallas frowned at Mason. "You got any idea where your client, John Leland, might have been today?"

"Come on, Ray." Mason waved a hand at the smoke across the clearing. "You don't think he had anything to do with this!"

"Why wouldn't I consider the possibility, if, as it looks, it turns out somebody set it."

Mason said, "You heard what the chief said. *If* it was set, it was probably the work of a firebug or a vandal. You have absolutely nothing that would involve Leland in this."

Dallas shrugged. "Not yet, maybe. But we'll see. Meanwhile, here's Anne Kimbro."

Mason turned as Anne Kimbro reached them. She stood silently for a moment, looking at the devastation of the fire before she asked anxiously, "There was no one inside the house, was there?"

Dallas answered her, "Not as far as we know."

"Does anyone know how the fire started?"

Dallas shook his head. "They haven't determined that yet. Let me get Chief Stacy. You can talk to him."

When Dallas walked away, Anne Kimbro looked at Mason curiously. "How did you know about the fire?"

"The lieutenant phoned me."

"I see." She thought for a moment. "Does that mean they think the fire is somehow connected to the murder of Iris? I mean, is that why he'd call you?"

Mason said, "I don't think they necessarily think that yet. But on the off chance that it might, yes, that's why the lieutenant let me know."

She said, "I see," again.

The fire had attracted to the scene a small group of people who lived nearby or were driving by in their cars.

The sun had set. It was getting dark. Men from the emergency service vehicles had set up giant, generator-powered floodlights around the perimeters of the clearing. Suddenly, the whole scene was lighted up brighter than day, the lights reflecting off the glistening rubber coats of the firemen sifting through the rubble. All that was left standing of the house was the now-smoke-blackened stone fireplace and the chimney rising more than two stories into the air above where the roof had been. As the last of the smoke thinned and trailed away in ragged wisps, the fireplace and chimney were illuminated in the floodlights like a stark etching of an ancient totem.

Mason and Anne stood watching silently until Dallas returned with Chief Stacy. Dallas introduced the battalion chief to Anne Kimbro.

Stacy looked at Anne. "I wonder if you'd mind answering a couple of questions for me?"

She nodded. "Not at all."

"No one lived here, is that right?"

"That's right. We—I—was renovating the house up until recently. It hasn't been occupied for years. The house had been left to my mother, and she left it to me."

Stacy was making notes. He asked, "Can you think of anything in the house that might have accidentally caused the fire? I mean, do you know whether there were any unusually inflammable materials stored anywhere inside?"

"No. Not that I know of."

"Been any reports of any suspicious strangers—any strangers—in the area?"

"No. I haven't heard of any."

Chief Stacy glanced up from the notes he was writing. "How about insurance? You had insurance on the house? The usual insurance?"

"Yes," she said. "We've always carried insurance on the house. The homeowners' policy, as far as I know, covering damage, theft, fire."

"I don't suppose you have any idea how the fire might have started?"

Anne looked at him carefully. "No, of course I don't. How could I?"

"All right, Miss Kimbro. Thank you. If we have any more questions, I'll contact you. Lieutenant Dallas here has told me where I can reach you."

Anne said, "I have a question to ask you, Chief. Have your men had a chance to make sure there was no one trapped in the fire?"

"They've determined there were no fatalities," Stacy said.

Anne looked at Dallas and then at Mason. "If there's no reason for me to stay any longer, I'll be leaving."

"There's no reason for you to stay," Dallas told her.

Mason nodded. He said, "Anne, try to get some rest.

You've had your share of shocks lately. I'll be in touch with you."

After she'd gone, Chief Stacy said, "She strikes me as a very self-assured young lady." He looked at Dallas. "She's not a suspect in the murder that happened here, is she?"

"No," Dallas said. "We've already made an arrest in the case."

"As soon as we've completed our investigation of the fire, I'll let you know," Stacy said, and walked away.

Mason and Dallas started back to where their cars were parked.

Dallas said, "Look, Perry, I'm going to want to talk to John Leland. Tomorrow. My office. At noon."

"I'm telling you, Ray, he had nothing to do with this fire. I'm sure of it."

"Yeah, well," Dallas said, "I want to be sure of it, too. It looks like somebody had a reason for burning the place down. Offhand, I can't think of a better motive than that somebody did it to destroy any evidence we might have overlooked in the murder of Iris Jantzen." Dallas pointed a finger. "Tomorrow. My office. At noon."

Mason opened the door of his car and got in. He said, "You just can't consider the possibility that someone other than Leland might have had that motive, can you?"

Mason slammed the car door and drove away.

13

"How was your weekend, Paul?" Mason asked.

Mason had stepped into Drake's office the next morning on his way to his own office just down the hallway.

"Well, counting the time I spent out in the rain on Friday night, watching the house where that guy, Newcombe, lives, and waiting for him to return home, and the other two days I spent tramping around Coldwater Canyon trying to locate witnesses, it wasn't exactly a fun-filled weekend."

"I thought you were going to put some of your other operatives to work on the case."

"I did," Drake said. "But I can only work them in shifts, and when someone has to relieve them, I'm the one. Actually, I don't mind, Perry. You know me. I only get bugged when none of our efforts pay off."

"It was that bad?"

Drake nodded. "For instance, when I first went to talk to Newcombe, there was nobody home. I waited around for a while, then I went knocking on doors on both sides of his house, to see if anyone knew where he might be. I told his neighbors I was an insurance assessor. Most of the people on the block knew him, but none of them knew where he might be. The word I got was that he frequently disappeared for days at a time. Naturally, that intrigued me. One of the neighbors mentioned Newcombe had a dog, and he boarded the dog at a kennel when he went away on trips. We checked out all the kennels in that part of town until we found the dog. The kennel owner said Newcombe told him he'd be back Tuesday or Wednesday. I'll keep checking until he shows up. The fact is, I have a hunch Newcombe is something of an oddball."

"Okay, Paul. What about your forays in Coldwater Canyon?"

Drake pushed his chair back and braced his feet against the edge of the desk. "Not much better luck there. Except I did talk to this one woman who lives right across the road from Anne Kimbro's house. A Mrs. Mary Domley. She did see a car turn into the road to Anne Kimbro's place late in the afternoon of the murder. She says a woman was driving the car. At the time, she says she assumed it was Anne Kimbro. She's seen her at other times."

"It was probably Iris," Mason said. "Did she say what time it was?"

"I asked her. She said she couldn't be certain."

"Then I don't see how she would be of much use to the prosecution, either."

"My thoughts exactly," Drake said. "One other interesting piece of information about Mrs. Domley. She's lived out there for years. She was living there at the time of the other murder, twenty years ago. She remembers Edward Larner and Elizabeth Jantzen, and said she used to see them coming and going before that murder."

"Anything else?"

"That's about it for now. We still haven't been able to get any kind of lead on Harold Fadden, the guy Iris was supposed to have tried to blackmail. Looks like he got out of the pen and walked off the edge of the earth, without leaving a trail. Listen, what about the fire at that house last night? They had a mention of it on the news on TV this morning."

Mason said, "There's not much to tell. I was out there early last evening. Ray Dallas tipped me off about the fire."

Mason recounted the events that had taken place at the house in Coldwater Canyon. He concluded, "Dallas wants to question Leland about the fire. Dallas has some kind of theory Leland might have burned the place down to destroy evidence against him that the police might have overlooked."

Drake raised an eyebrow. "And you don't think he did, is that it?"

"What I think," Mason said, "is that Carter Phillips and Ray Dallas have so much pressure on them to put John Leland away for the murder of Iris Jantzen that at this point they'll hang any charge they can find on him." Mason stood. "And I'm not going to let them get away with it." He shook his head. "Here I am, trying to prepare for Leland's preliminary hearing in court tomorrow, and now Dallas wants Leland in his office at noon today to question him about last night's fire. And of course they know I'm going to be there with him."

Mason started toward the door. "Let me know if Newcombe shows up. I'd like to have a talk with him myself."

"Will do," Drake said.

Mason went out and down the hall to his office. Della was waiting by his desk, and took his briefcase to empty it.

She said, "Carter Phillips phoned you. He said it was important that he talk to you before the end of the day, but that he'd be in court this morning and in the early afternoon. He said he'd call you when he was free. He asked that you call him if you're going to be out of the office in the afternoon."

"Fine, thanks, Della. Phillips probably is going to ask if we'll plea-bargain before the hearing begins."

Della looked at him, frowning. "Doesn't he know you've never plea-bargained a client?"

"Of course he does! If that's the question he has in mind, it would be his way of trying to get under my skin, make me think his case is stronger than I believe it is."

"Come to think of it, it sounds like something D.A. Phillips would do," Della agreed.

Mason had begun pacing the office, his face thoughtful.

Della, attuned to his moods, looked at him anxiously. "Something troubling you, Chief?"

He told her about the fire in Coldwater Canyon the evening before. He said, "I phoned John Leland early this morning, and directed him to be at headquarters at noon today, saying that I'd be there. It was something he said when I told him Dallas wanted to question him about the fire, that Dallas would want to know where he had been at the time the fire started. What Leland said was, 'Oh, I know how to take care of that,' and then he hung up."

"What do you think he meant?"

Mason shook his head. "That's what bothers me. I don't know what he meant. I tried to call him back, and the line was busy. I kept trying, and the line was still busy, and then there was no answer."

Mason stopped pacing and sat at his desk. He spread out the papers Della had taken from his briefcase. "We'll just have to wait and see what happens at noon. Between now and then I want to dictate the notes I'll need with me in court tomorrow. You can type them up while I'm at headquarters with Leland and Dallas."

14

Officer Molly Gilmore, sitting at her desk outside Lieutenant Dallas's office, glanced up as Perry Mason approached.

"You can go right in, Mr. Mason," she said. "He's expecting you."

"Thank you, Molly. My client, John Leland, is supposed to be here, too."

"The lieutenant told me. He hasn't arrived yet. I'll send him in."

"Thanks."

Mason tapped on the office door and went in.

Dallas was sitting at his desk. He was in his shirtsleeves and was wearing his shoulder harness and holster, the holster empty, his coat slung over the back of the chair.

Dallas pushed his chair back as Mason sat down.

"You're right on time, Perry," Dallas said, glancing at his watch. "Even if your client isn't."

Just as Mason said, "He'll be here," there was a tap on the door.

Dallas called out, "Come on in."

The door opened and John Leland walked in, looking, for a moment, apprehensive, until he saw Mason.

Leland glanced at Dallas, then Mason. "Mr. Mason. Lieutenant."

Dallas waved a hand. "Have a seat, Mr. Leland." Dallas pulled his chair closer to the desk. "You know why I wanted to see you today?"

Leland nodded. "Mr. Mason told me about the fire last night."

"Were you anywhere near that house yesterday?"

"No, sir."

"When was the last time you were there?"

"When Mr. Mason and I were there a few days ago."

"And you haven't been back there alone?"

"No, sir. I wouldn't have gone back there at all if Mr. Mason hadn't asked me to go."

"Where were you yesterday," Dallas asked, "between the hours of five and six P.M.?"

"I was home, in my apartment, all afternoon and last evening."

"Alone, I suppose," Dallas said, as if that were the foregone answer.

Leland shook his head. "Actually, I wasn't alone, no."

Dallas was clearly surprised. "Oh, someone was with you? I'd certainly like to know who it was."

"I thought you might, sir."

Leland went quickly to the door, opened it, and beckoned.

Ginny Rollins, Leland's secretary, walked in, her lips

fixed in a tremulous smile. Leland motioned her to the chair where he had been sitting, and he sat in the chair next to her.

Mason continued to observe the proceedings silently.

"Ah! Miss Rollins," Dallas said. "Mr. Leland has informed you why I wanted to question him today?"

Ginny Rollins nodded.

Dallas leaned forward toward her. "Mr. Leland tells me you and he were together yesterday."

Ginny Rollins wet her lips. "Yes, sir. We were."

"At his apartment?"

"Yes."

Dallas nodded solemnly, pulled a pad of paper toward him, and picked up a pen. He wrote on the pad for several seconds before he looked up. "What time was that? The exact time you were with Mr. Leland at his apartment yesterday."

Ginny Rollins looked at Leland, looked back at the lieutenant.

"As well as I can remember," she said, "it was from somewhere around four o'clock to close to seven, seven o'clock."

"P.M.?"

She appeared confused. "P.M.? Yes, in the late afternoon, early evening. Isn't that what we're talking about?" She glanced at Leland for reassurance. He had his eyes on Dallas.

Dallas said sharply, "What we're talking about, Miss Rollins, is the time you were with Mr. Leland in his apartment yesterday." He tapped the writing pad. "This is an official police report. We want the report to be accurate. To be accurate, I need you to tell me whether the time you were with Mr. Leland yesterday in his apartment was A.M. or P.M."

"Four o'clock to seven o'clock, P.M." she said, her voice hesitant.

Leland said quickly, "We were bringing some of our office accounts up to date, Lieutenant. I've been away from work so much lately, answering these endless questions, that we haven't had time to keep up with the bookkeeping. Ginny, Miss Rollins, offered to come to my place yesterday, Sunday, to help us catch up."

Dallas was frowning. He looked as if he was about to ask another question.

Mason spoke up. "Lieutenant, I believe you informed me that the reason you wanted to question Mr. Leland today was to verify the whereabouts of Mr. Leland during a specific period of time yesterday. It appears to me that he's complied with your request, with the kind assistance of Miss Rollins. You have both their statements. I can't see why they should be detained any longer."

Dallas considered Mason's words for a moment before he shrugged. He looked at Leland and Ginny Rollins. "All right, you can leave now."

As Mason, Leland, and Ginny Rollins stood, Dallas raised a hand. "I must advise you, Mr. Leland, Miss Rollins, you may be questioned about this matter again, at a later date." He added, "Mr. Mason, I'd like you to remain for a moment, alone."

Mason nodded and turned to Leland, "Please wait for me outside."

When the office door closed behind Leland and Ginny Rollins, Dallas, standing, leaned forward, both hands on the desk. "Perry, I wouldn't want to think you knew anything in advance about this little charade we just witnessed being performed here. It's clear that young lady is so smitten with your client she'd do almost anything he asked her to, including providing him with an alibi."

"Ray, Ray," Mason said mildly, "do you think I'd be a party to encouraging the giving of false testimony?"

"Maybe not precisely that," Dallas said dryly. "No. But what I do think is that you will do almost anything you can get away with to protect your clients. And sometimes I think you skate on pretty thin legal ice."

"That's my job," Mason said, his voice still mild, "as I see it. Especially if my clients are innocent, and until the law—*the law, Ray*—can prove otherwise."

Mason paused, had another thought, and said, "I don't even rest my case for the defense on the more or less generally accepted wisdom that it's better that a dozen —or whatever number—of guilty persons to go free than that one innocent person should be convicted. Although I do believe that, for me there's more. In my mind, as I always say, in a murder case, if the wrong person is convicted, then the person who is really guilty has claimed not just one victim, but two; justice has been thwarted twice."

"All right, all right," Dallas said gruffly, "I let you make your point. Getting back to Leland, the funny thing about our talk today is that he reminded me of something I'd completely forgotten."

"What's that?"

"I'd completely forgotten that since the murder, you and he had visited the scene again."

"At the time, I told you we were going to," Mason said.

Dallas nodded. "Yeah. But I'd forgotten. Remembering makes me feel even more strongly that he could have set the fire—the day he was there with you, he may have noticed a piece of evidence we'd overlooked."

"But he wasn't at the house yesterday," Mason pointed out. "He's told you that. And he has a witness, Ginny Rollins, to back him up."

"And I'm telling you here and now, I'm going to try to discredit that witness, prove she's lying. If I do, I'm going to nail them both for obstruction of justice, at the very least."

Mason was leaving. "Prove it," he said.

John Leland was waiting in the outer office. Ginny Rollins was nowhere in sight, but Anne Kimbro was there, sitting stiffly in a chair on the opposite side of the room from Leland, neither of them looking at the other.

As Mason approached Leland, police officer Molly Gilmore called out, "Miss Kimbro, Lieutenant Dallas will see you now."

Mason took Leland by the arm and led him out of the building, Leland asking him, "What's Anne doing here?"

"Dallas probably wants to question her about the fire." Mason tugged at Leland's arm. "Come on."

"But Anne didn't even speak to me!" Leland protested.

Mason, exasperated, said, "Right now, you'd better be worried about more important matters than that."

Out on the street Mason swung Leland around so they were face to face. "Listen to me," Mason said, his voice harsh. "I don't know what you think you're up to—and I don't want to know—but Dallas suspects that story you and Ginny told him is complete hogwash. He's going all out to prove she's lying to protect you. If he succeeds, that alone will give him a pretty good circumstantial case against you for arson, if not worse. You try to play smart with the cops, Leland, and you'll outsmart yourself every time."

Leland looked shaken, but he said hoarsely, "I wasn't out at that house yesterday. I didn't set the fire. I was in my apartment all afternoon and last evening. That's the truth."

When Mason didn't say anything, Leland said, "If I'd been there alone, who would believe me?"

When Mason still didn't say anything, Leland added, "So I guess you can say I was lucky she was there with me. And nobody can prove otherwise."

Mason put his hand on Leland's shoulder. "Go home, John. Stay there tonight. I'll see you in court tomorrow."

Mason returned to his office, where Della, standing at his desk, was holding the telephone to her ear. She saw Mason and said into the telephone, "Hold on, please. I'll see if he's available."

She put her hand over the mouthpiece. "It's D.A. Phillips, Chief. Do you want to talk to him?"

Mason reached out and took the phone. "This is Mason."

Della, arranging papers on the desk, kept an eye on Mason on the phone as he listened briefly, said, "Yes, I spoke with him. . . . Yes . . . If the judge granted the order, I'll be there. . . . Yes . . . All right. Good-bye."

He slammed the phone down, shaking his head.

"What was that all about?" Della asked.

"Carter Phillips has pulled a fast one," Mason said. "Remember, I told you that old man Jantzen had a theory about a motive Leland might have had for killing Iris? I said it wouldn't do Carter Phillips any good, because Jantzen was too ill to testify in court." Mason shook his head again. "Well, I underestimated our esteemed D.A. He got an order from the judge to allow Jantzen to testify on videotape at his home with the provision that I be allowed to cross-examine on the tape. He ruled the tape could be played in court. I have to go out to Jantzen's house now."

Della indicated the papers she had arranged on the

desk. "I typed up the notes you wanted for court to-morrow."

Mason handed her his briefcase. "Pack them up for me, please, Della. I'll review them tonight after we do the tape."

Della said, "You know what I think, Perry? I think you fight hardest when the odds are all against you."

She made Mason laugh then; she said, "Of course, the kinds of cases you take to defend, when are the odds ever not against you?"

15

A crowd of TV newsmen, cameras, and newspaper and radio reporters were waiting on the steps of the courthouse in the rain when Mason arrived with John Leland. Della Street and Paul Drake, Jr., trailed behind Mason and Leland into the building, Mason fending off questions shouted at him with an affable "No comment" and a cheerful smile on his face.

Inside the courtroom Mason led Leland to the defense table. Della and Drake took seats in the first row of chairs directly behind Mason. The reporters who had been outside hurried down the aisles to take places in the press section. The murder of Iris Jantzen had been the lead news story in the media for the past several days, and all the seats were taken by curious spectators.

Judge Samuel Maynard entered from a side door at

the front of the courtroom and took his place on the bench.

The bailiff pounded a gavel and declared the court to be in session.

Mason took a moment, while Judge Maynard was settling himself behind the bench, to glance around the courtroom. He saw that Joseph Larner was there, and a few seats away from him was Ginny Rollins. Mason noticed there were several other familiar faces present— one of the patrolmen who had been at the house in Coldwater canyon the night of the murder, Lieutenant Ray Dallas, two homicide detectives, a couple of members of the forensic unit, and the medical examiner. Most of them would be witnesses for the prosecution.

Judge Maynard announced that this was the time heretofore fixed for the preliminary hearing in the case of the People versus Leland, and asked if the defense and the prosecution were ready to proceed.

"Ready for the prosecution," Carter Phillips replied.

"Ready for the defendant, Your Honor," Mason said.

Judge Maynard, tall, broad-shouldered, his hair streaked with gray, and wearing faintly tinted eyeglasses, turned toward Carter Phillips. "Call your first witness."

While the clerk was swearing in Patrolman Martin Eggers, Mason said softly to John Leland, who sat stiffly beside him, "Take a deep breath, John. The roller coaster ride's about to begin. Hang on with me; we'll get to the end, a bit shaken up from time to time, no doubt, but with any luck able to walk away when it's over."

D.A. Phillips moved toward the witness stand. "Officer Eggers, would you tell the court the events of the night of May eleventh, with regard to the murder of Iris Jantzen?"

Patrolman Eggers responded carefully, stating that he

and his partner, Patrolman Pete Delfin, had been directed by the police dispatcher to the house in Coldwater Canyon after there had been a phone call to the 911 emergency number, reporting a homicide. He said they were met at the front door of the house by a man who had identified himself as John Leland.

Eggers paused when the D.A. asked the patrolman to point out Leland. Eggers identified him.

The patrolman then continued his testimony. He said Leland had led them to the back of the house, where the victim's body lay. The victim had been stabbed in the back with a pair of gardening shears.

Phillips asked quickly, "What were your feelings at that time about the defendant? How did you view him?"

"Objection, Your Honor!" Mason interrupted before Eggers could answer. "Calls for an opinion on the part of the witness."

"I'll sustain, Mr. Mason." Judge Maynard waved a hand at Phillips. "Proceed."

"Then did you," Phillips asked, "notice anything unusual about the appearance of the defendant, John Leland?"

"Yes, sir. He had a handkerchief with a lot of blood on it wrapped around his hand. His left hand."

"Did you question him?"

"I tried to, but he wouldn't answer."

"Continue."

"My partner called the station house to report the circumstances. Then we waited until the homicide unit arrived to take over the investigation."

Phillips brought a series of photographs to the witness stand. "Officer Eggers, have you examined these photographs taken of the sunroom on the night of the murder?"

"I have. They show the scene as I saw it."

The D.A. noted that the photographs had been seen by the defense, and asked that they be introduced in evidence. Mason consented.

The D.A. took a step back. He nodded to Mason. "Cross-examine."

Mason, still seated, asked, "Officer Eggers, when you attempted to question Mr. Leland, as you've testified, did he tell you why he wouldn't answer your questions?"

"Yes, sir. He said he'd been advised not to answer any questions until you, his lawyer, were present."

"No further questions," Mason said.

As Patrolman Eggers stepped down, Carter Phillips called, as his next witness, Dr. James Lee, chief medical examiner for Los Angeles County.

Carter Phillips stood on the far side of the witness stand, so the judge would have an unobstructed view.

"Dr. Lee, you performed the autopsy on Iris Jantzen, did you not?"

The medical examiner, a solemn man, tall, thin, bald-headed, in his sixties, said, "I did."

"Would you tell the court the results of your findings?"

The doctor delivered his testimony in short, precise sentences, with no inflection in his voice. Mason, listening, thought again, as he often had during the years he had spent in court, how an expert witness, such as the medical examiner, always sounded programmed when giving testimony. All was as impersonal as a recording of a memorized script.

Dr. Lee stated that the victim had been killed by a stab wound. The pointed blades of a pair of gardening shears had penetrated into the left ventricle, or chamber, of the victim's heart. Death was instantaneous. The victim had been struck from behind, the pointed blades driven into the back between the fourth and fifth ribs before penetrating the left ventricle. Tear wounds of the flesh were consistent with the trajectory of the blades of the shears found embedded in the body. Only one blow was struck. The body showed no other external or internal injuries. The time of death was between 5:00 and 6:15 P.M., May 11, this year.

"You say only one blow was struck, Dr. Lee," D.A. Phillips said.

"Yes. One blow."

"Could you, from the angle of the stab wound, determine which hand the assailant used to stab the victim?"

"It could have been either hand," the medical examiner said. "Most likely, however, it was the left hand."

"The left hand," Carter Phillips repeated. "Why most likely the left hand?"

"The victim was struck on the left side of the back." Dr. Lee demonstrated with his hand. "It is my opinion that the blow was struck by an assailant using the left hand."

"Thank you, Doctor."

Mason walked forward. "Dr. Lee, you did testify that the blow could have been struck by the assailant using either hand?"

"Yes."

"You were aware, were you not, before appearing here today, that the defendant was left-handed?"

"I think I heard that. Yes."

Mason nodded. "Now, Doctor, would you demonstrate for the court how you believe the victim was attacked."

Mason signaled to Della Street, and she came forward.

Dr. Lee appeared puzzled as he started to rise, looking over at Carter Phillips questioningly. The D.A. was on his feet, but had not yet objected.

Mason said, "Doctor, this is my, secretary, Miss Street. I think you will agree that she is approximately the same height and weight as the victim?"

"All right, yes."

"Using her as a stand-in for the victim, would you please show the court the manner in which you believe she was attacked."

Dr. Lee stepped down from the witness stand, approached Della from behind, and made a stabbing motion with his left hand.

"Now, try it with your right hand," Mason said.

The medical examiner made another stabbing motion at Della's back, his hand twisted awkwardly, to touch the same spot on Della's body.

"I see," Mason said. "It does appear, according to your demonstration, that the killer would have more likely been left-handed." He looked at Dr. Lee. "You may return to the witness stand."

Mason saw that D.A. Phillips had sat down again.

Mason turned toward the courtroom and motioned to Drake. Drake brought one of the courtroom chairs and placed it in front of the witness stand.

Mason handed Dr. Lee a copy of the photograph of the sunroom taken at the time of Iris Jantzen's murder. He said, "You will note, Dr. Lee, that in this photograph there is clearly evident a chair that was in the sunroom —you see it?"

"I see it." The medical examiner was frowning again.

Della sat in the courtroom chair. Mason walked up behind her. He said, "Now, Doctor, let's assume the victim was sitting down at the time of the attack."

Mason made a stabbing motion with his right hand, then put both his hands under her arms and lifted her gently from the chair. He said, "Can you see how easily the assailant could have killed the victim in this manner, and then could have stretched the body out on the floor where it was found?"

"Objection, Your Honor! Objection!" Carter Phillips was sputtering the words. "This demonstration by the defense is immaterial and irrelevant."

Judge Maynard leaned over the bench. "Mr. Mason?"

"Your Honor, I think that if the witness has based his testimony on one set of facts and has subsequently been presented another set of facts that he might not have taken into consideration, he should be able to answer my question."

"I'm inclined to agree." Judge Maynard nodded. "Objection overruled. The witness will answer the question."

"Yes," Dr. Lee said, "I suppose the victim could have been killed in such a fashion."

"In which case," Mason said quickly, "would it still be your opinion that, as you stated to the prosecutor, the blow was likely struck by an assailant using the left hand?"

Dr. Lee said, "I would have to state that *if* the victim was killed while sitting in the chair, I would not be able to form an opinion as to which hand the assailant used."

Mason nodded. "In other words, the assailant could have been either right-handed or left-handed?"

"That is correct."

Della stood up. Drake removed the chair.

Mason said, "Even if the victim had been stabbed while seated and the chair placed in another part of the room, the chair would likely have had the victim's bloodstains on it, wouldn't you think?"

"I would think so." Dr. Lee nodded.

"Isn't it true, Doctor, that as medical examiner, you have seen all the forensic evidence gathered in this case?"

"I have."

"Tell me," Mason put the question slowly, "did you anywhere in the forensic evidence report see that the chair in the sunroom was examined for traces of the victim's blood?"

"I did not, no. There was no such evidence recorded."

"In other words, there was no report that the chair had been examined?"

"No."

"No, it was not examined?"

"No."

"A pity." Mason turned away. "An oversight, no doubt. And, unfortunately, we all know the chair was destroyed in the subsequent fire that consumed the house where the murder occurred."

"Your Honor!" Carter Phillips protested. "Defense counsel is making a speech."

Judge Maynard pointed his gavel at the D.A. "Mr. Prosecutor, may I remind you, this is not a jury trial. The court is quite competent to know when a speech is being made."

"Yes, Your Honor," Phillips said.

The judge aimed his gavel at Mason. "Mr. Mason, you will refrain from further comments."

Mason said, "Yes, Your Honor."

Mason turned back to the witness stand. "I have no further questions."

At the defense table as Mason sat down, Drake leaned forward. "You finessed that one neatly, Perry."

"I doubt that I convinced the judge of anything," Mason said softly. "But as he pointed out, there was no jury present. If we go to trial, there will be. I'm trying to send a message to the prosecution that a lot of its evidence is circumstantial, and we can raise strong issues of reasonable doubt that a jury will have to consider."

Carter Phillips called Lieutenant Ray Dallas to the stand.

Mason made notes as Dallas testified.

The lieutenant stated that when he went to the house—"the murder scene," as he put it—was as had been described in the testimony of Patrolman Eggers. The D.A. produced the photographs of the sunroom, and Dallas agreed they reflected what he had seen. Dallas went on to recount that after Perry Mason had arrived at the house, Leland had given a statement relating his actions there before Patrolmen Eggers and Delfin got there.

Phillips asked, "Do you have a copy of that statement?"

"Yes, sir, I have." Dallas held up some papers.

The D.A. took time out to deliver copies of the statement to the judge and to Mason.

Phillips returned to face Dallas. "Would you please read to the court Mr. Leland's statement."

Dallas read the account Mason had heard Leland give on the night of the murder. When Dallas had concluded, the D.A. asked that the statement be entered into the record. Mason so stipulated.

"Turning now to another matter," Phillips said, addressing Dallas, "we have heard testimony from Patrolman Eggers that the defendant, John Leland, had a handkerchief with blood on it wrapped around his hand that night. Did you also have occasion to note this fact?"

"I did."

Phillips nodded. "The defendant stated to you in the account he gave, which you have just read to the court, that he injured his hand when he had to smash the glass in the door in order to enter the sunroom. My question is, Which hand was it that he had injured?"

"His left hand."

"His left hand," Phillips repeated. "Yes. Now, did anything else occur during the search of the room that night with regard to the fact that Mr. Leland used his left hand to smash the glass in the door?"

"We found a single gardener's glove in the sunroom, lying under a wheelbarrow. A right-handed glove."

"And the left-handed glove was missing?"

"Objection!" Mason interjected. "Objection, Your Honor! The prosecutor is attempting to draw a conclusion without a foundation of facts. There has been no evidence presented to establish a connection between John Leland and some missing glove."

Before Judge Maynard could rule, D.A. Phillips said smoothly, "Your Honor, this witness has not been asked to draw a conclusion. My examination is designed to put into the record the sequence of the police investigation on the night of the murder, and subsequently."

The judge frowned. "Let the record show that on the basis of the prosecutor's just-stated premise, the defense's objection is overruled. However, Mr. Mason, I may entertain an exception to this ruling at a later point, if you choose to raise the issue."

Mason nodded. "Thank you, Your Honor."

Phillips said, "If I may continue, *for the purpose of putting into the record the sequence of the police investigation subsequent to the night of the murder*, did you, Lieutenant Dallas, find the missing left-handed glove at a later date?"

"Objection," Mason said wearily. "Your Honor, please let the record show that the defense again objects on the same grounds as the previous objection raised to this line of questioning."

Judge Maynard glanced at the court reporter. "Let the

record so note. And note as well that the court overrules the defense objection with the same stipulation as in the previous ruling. Continue, Mr. Phillips."

This time Phillips said, "Thank you, Your Honor." He turned toward the witness stand. "Did you, Lieutenant Dallas, find the missing left-handed glove at a later date?"

Dallas was clearly enjoying the exchanges between the prosecutor and Mason. "Yes, sir, we did. The glove was found during a later search of the murder scene. The glove had been stuffed into a crevice in the lower part of the chimney of the fireplace in the sunroom. The glove had bloodstains on it."

Phillips walked back to the prosecution table and picked up a sealed plastic packet.

He asked, "The spot where the glove was found would be a distance of approximately how far from the victim's body?"

"Not approximately," Dallas corrected, "but exactly six feet, two inches, away from the body. We measured the distance."

The D.A. carried the plastic packet to Dallas to examine. "This glove, Lieutenant?"

Dallas looked at the glove inside the plastic packet carefully. "Yes, sir. This is the glove. It has my identifying tag on it, placed there at the time of the discovery."

Phillips took the plastic packet back. He said, "We ask that this evidence be entered into the record as State Exhibit Five-A."

Mason said, "No objection."

There was a brief pause in the proceedings, while Carter Phillips transferred the plastic packet to the bailiff.

Mason turned sideways in his chair and motioned to Drake to lean forward.

"That's not the last we're going to see of that gardener's

glove," Mason told Drake. "Unless I miss my bet, Carter Phillips is going to try to make it his incriminating clue."

At the front of the courtroom Phillips addressed Lieutenant Dallas again.

"Moving on to another subject, Lieutenant, would you tell the court why you were called to the scene, in Coldwater Canyon, the night of the murder of Iris Jantzen? I mean, you're assigned to headquarters, and surely you don't personally investigate every homicide that occurs in the Greater Los Angeles area?"

Dallas nodded. "I'm called in on most homicides where unusual circumstances exist."

"And in the Iris Jantzen murder, what were those unusual circumstances?"

"There was the fact that a prior murder had been committed in the same house, twenty years earlier."

"I see." The D.A. frowned. "Yes, that would constitute unusual circumstances, I should think. Would you now brief the court on the facts of this prior murder of some twenty years ago."

Dallas sat back in his chair and related the account of the murder of Elizabeth Jantzen and of the hunt for Edward Larner. "It was one of the most celebrated murder cases ever to have occurred in Los Angeles," he concluded.

"On the night of the murder of Iris Jantzen, did you discover any connection between the murder of Iris Jantzen and the earlier murder of Elizabeth Jantzen?"

"If you mean other than the fact that both women were murdered in the same house, that both had been married to the same man, Benjamin Jantzen, and that the property had been left by Elizabeth Jantzen to her daughter, now legally named Anne Kimbro, no. I considered the two events to be, well, odd, but likely simply coincidence."

Phillips stepped closer to the witness box. "Did you later, in the course of your investigation of the murder of Iris Jantzen, discover yet another connection between the two cases?"

"Yes." Dallas looked out at the courtroom. "I discovered that the defendant, John Leland, who also had had his name legally changed, was in fact the son of Edward Larner, who to this day remains wanted for the murder of Elizabeth Jantzen."

D.A. Phillips swung around toward the judge. "I have no further questions for this witness for now, Your Honor."

Judge Maynard said, "Mr. Mason."

As Mason approached Ray Dallas, sitting patiently on the witness stand, the lawyer put out of his mind all considerations of a friendship between them. Here, each understood the other. They were professionals, committed to the jobs they had to do. Mason's only loyalty was to his client.

Mason asked his opening question.

"Lieutenant, you have testified that on the night of the murder of Iris Jantzen, you were placed in charge of the investigation because"—Mason glanced down at his notes—"quote, 'I'm called in on most homicides where unusual circumstances exist,' unquote. And, quote, 'There was the fact that a prior murder had been committed in the same house, twenty years earlier,' unquote. That was your testimony?"

"Yes, sir."

Mason nodded. "So, I take it that prior to the time you were actually in the house, it certainly must have been your feeling that there *was* a connection between the two murders. I mean, that's why you were placed in charge of the investigation. Was that your feeling?"

"Yes. I suppose it was."

"But once you were in the house, you no longer entertained the thought that there could be a connection between the earlier and later murders. Why was that?"

"I had a chance to observe the scene."

"To observe the scene? And what was the scene that made you so quickly discount the feeling you had had before?"

Dallas shifted in the chair. "There was the body, there was the defendant, who had been alone with the victim for a period of time, there were the gardening shears, which had been handy, there was his injured hand, and finally, by the defendant's own admission, there was the fact that he and the victim did not get along."

"Still," Mason said, "all circumstantial, wouldn't you say? Certainly nothing beyond a reasonable doubt?"

"Objection!" Carter Phillips was on his feet. "Calls for an opinion. The court will make that judgment."

"Sustained."

"In any event," Mason said, "you didn't widen your investigation beyond marshaling a body of circumstantial evidence against the defendant, isn't that true?"

"We considered other possibilities."

"Such as?"

"A review was made of all the known information in the earlier murder, the murder of Elizabeth Jantzen." Dallas spread his hands. "We could find nothing to connect the two cases."

Mason said, "I see. I'd hardly call that an investigation."

"Objection, Your Honor!" Carter Phillips protested.

"The lieutenant has answered the question. Mr. Mason is badgering the witness."

Mason turned to the judge. "I withdraw the last statement." He glanced down at his notes and then fixed his eyes on Dallas.

"You've testified to the left-handed gardener's glove, first missing and some time later discovered."

"Yes, sir."

"The significance of that glove, I take it, is that you knew, you know, that the defendant is left-handed. Is that correct?"

"It is," Dallas agreed.

"And do you have proof, any proof, to connect the defendant to that glove, either before it was missing or later, when it was found in the fireplace?"

"No. No physical link. The victim's blood type was, however, found on the missing glove."

"A glove," Mason said quickly, "that could have been worn by anyone at the time of the stabbing." Mason turned away.

"That's all," he said. "No further questions."

Judge Maynard glanced at the clock. He said, "The court has been given several lengthy statements that should be examined before this hearing proceeds. Therefore, we will adjourn until tomorrow morning at ten o'clock, by which time the court will have familiarized itself with all the details of the written statements. This court is adjourned."

The judge left the bench.

Mason began to assemble his notes to put into his briefcase.

Della Street came over. "Let me do that," she said. She picked up the notes and the briefcase.

John Leland looked at Mason anxiously. "The lieutenant sure made it sound like I'm guilty, didn't he? Listening to him explaining the way his investigation went, step by step, I can understand why the judge may decide I should be put on trial." He shook his head miserably.

"This is only round one," Mason said encouragingly. "There were no knockout punches delivered, so it's too early for a decision."

Mason turned and saw that Drake had left the courtroom.

"Where's Paul?" he asked Della.

"He said he had to make a phone call. He said he'd be right back."

"Find him for me," Mason said. "I need him right now."

Della left. Mason finished putting his notes into the briefcase.

"Is it all right if I leave now?" Leland asked.

"Stick around for a minute. I want to speak with Drake. Then we'll leave."

Della returned, Drake right behind her.

Mason stood and went to Drake before Drake reached the table. "I need to talk to you, Paul. I don't want Leland to hear."

Drake nodded.

"When Leland leaves, I want him tailed. I want a man watching him around the clock. He's scared, and I don't want him to run away a second time."

"Got it," Drake said. "One of my operatives, Jesse Carmody, is right outside. I'll put him on it."

Drake put a restraining hand on Mason's arm. "Listen, I just called into the office. There was a message. The man I've had watching Newcombe's house reported in that Newcombe had returned but looked like he was about to take off again."

"All right, Paul. Let's you and I go out there and have a talk with Newcombe before *he* flies the coop. I may want him to testify. I'll get a subpoena issued for him, and we'll take it with us."

Mason returned to the defense table, where Leland was waiting.

"Okay, John. You can go on home now. I'll see you here in court tomorrow at ten A.M."

The reporters and newsmen would be waiting outside in front of the courthouse. Mason had made arrangements for Leland to leave by a side entrance, and Della went with him. Drake's operative, Carmody, would be waiting unobtrusively near the side entrance, and Leland would be under surveillance until he was due back in court.

16

As Mason, Drake, and Drake's operative, Sam Baylor,
approached the front steps of the house where Bernard
Newcombe lived, Baylor—who had had the house under
surveillance—warned, "Watch it now, guys. Given half
a chance, that dog he's got will chew your arm or leg
off."

The house was a small bungalow with a couple of
dusty palm trees on either side of the front porch. The
front door was open behind a screen door.

From inside the house there was the sound of deep-
throated growls, and before Mason could set foot on the
porch, a man appeared behind the screen door.

"Hold it right there, mister! Who are you? What do
you want?"

The dog threw itself against the inside of the screen
door, snarling, and the man yanked it back on a leash.

Drake had his raincoat and jacket open, his hand on the revolver in his shoulder holster.

Mason stood on the top step and said, "Mr. Newcombe, my name's Perry Mason. I'm a lawyer. These are my associates. I'd like to have a word with you about your troubles with the Jantzens and Questall Pharmaceuticals. I'll only take a minute of your time. It could be to your advantage."

"Nothing about that bunch has ever been to my advantage."

"Well, maybe I can offer you another chance," Mason said. "At least you can hear me out on what I have to say."

Mason wiped the rain from his face with his hand. "Can we talk on the porch? We're getting soaked out here."

"All right, come on up." The man disappeared briefly, taking the dog with him, then reappeared, opening the screen door and stepping out on the porch. The dog continued to snarl and growl from somewhere in the house.

Bernard Newcombe was a skinny man of medium height. Most of his hair was gone, except for a few yellowish-white strands plastered across the top of his skull. Mason judged him to be in his seventies.

"I'm not here representing the Jantzens or Questall," Mason said.

Newcombe looked at Mason with narrowed eyes. "I know who you are, Mason. You're defending the fellow they say murdered that Jantzen woman. What's it got to do with me?"

Mason said, "As part of the defense of my client, I'm trying to find out all I can about the Jantzens, particularly Iris Jantzen. I know you had several lawsuits against them and their company. I'd like to know the details of your lawsuits; it just might be helpful to me and to my client."

Newcombe shook his head. "I don't see how anything I'd tell you could be helpful. Besides, why should I want to tell you anything?"

Mason nodded. "I can see where you might think that. Still, I can't see where you'd have anything to lose by telling me the story of your problem with them."

"I know you lawyers and your tricks, Mason. You want to make them look bad so your client looks better. I tell you my story, and the next thing I know, you haul me into court to tell it again, and there I am, involved in something that has nothing to do with me, however much it might help you."

"If that happens," Mason pointed out reasonably, "at least it gives you another chance to tell your story in a courtroom. For now, however, all I want you to do is tell me about your lawsuits here and now."

"No, sir!" Newcombe shook his head vigorously. "I don't want to get involved with them people anymore. Besides, I have plans to be away. I got no time to spend in court."

"Mr. Newcombe," Mason said, his voice suddenly hard, "like it or not, you *are* involved. This is a murder case. I've tried to give you a chance to talk to me today." Mason reached into his coat pocket, took out the subpoena, and jammed it into Newcombe's hand. "Since you refuse, this is a subpoena to appear in court. You'll talk to me then, or you won't just spend time in court; you'll spend it in jail."

Mason turned away. "Let's go," he said to Drake and Sam Baylor.

"Hey! Hold on!" Newcombe called out. "All right, I'll talk to you."

Mason went back up on the porch, again wiping the rain off his face.

Newcombe looked deflated, all the feistiness gone out of him. He said, "The minute you showed up here, I should have known I was going to get involved in this whole business.

"In fact," Mason pointed out, "you knew from the time Iris Jantzen was murdered that sooner or later there would be questions asked of you, didn't you? After the lawsuits you brought."

"I reckon I did." Newcombe sighed. "Well, what do you want to know?"

"Tell me about this problem you and your wife had with Questall."

"It was poor Clara had the problem. First, she was having trouble sleeping, and high blood pressure, dragging around all day, feeling terrible. There was this new drug came out along with a lot of fancy advertising guaranteeing it would help you sleep. Clara saw the ads and started taking the pills. Questall made them. The product was called Resterin. She only took one bottle of them. At first they seemed to quiet her down, but then it happened."

Newcombe shook his head. "In the middle of the night, one night, she had a seizure, like. She had trouble breathing, she couldn't speak, her left arm and leg were paralyzed. I called an ambulance, and they rushed her to the hospital. They said she'd had a stroke. In the next couple of days they gave her all kinds of tests, and they still said she'd had a stroke. They kept her in the hospital for a week, and a funny thing happened. Little by little, her symptoms cleared up. Her breathing, her speech, her arm and leg that had been paralyzed."

Newcombe shook his head again. "At first the doctors

didn't know what to make of what was happening. They decided it wasn't a stroke, after all. What had happened to her had mimicked a stroke. They took a lot more tests, and finally they decided her condition had been caused by the medication she'd taken, those Resterin pills."

Mason interrupted. "Had they been prescribed by a doctor?"

"They were a prescription drug, yeah. Well, I guess it should have been a relief to know that Clara hadn't really had a stroke. But it cost us all the savings we had, and besides, Clara was never the same afterward. She wouldn't go anywhere, was scared to death all the time. See, she was sure it was going to happen to her again without warning. She couldn't get it into her head that she really hadn't had a stroke. We went to see a lawyer, to see if we could sue somebody about the pills. At first the lawyer thought we could sue the doctor that gave her the pills. But he had died meanwhile, and didn't leave any money."

Newcombe looked out at the rain and back at Mason. "So then this lawyer we'd hired decided we'd sue the drug company, Questall. He said there'd been other cases similar to Clara's where the party had won big sums of money, not against Questall, but against other big companies. It took a couple of years before we went to court. Our lawyer had had several doctors examine Clara, and then, too, we had all the hospital reports from the time Clara had her seizure. It was a jury trial, and even though the company had pulled the pills off the market by then, we won. A million dollars, they said we'd get. That perked Clara up a lot."

"I would think so," Mason said.

"But it didn't happen," Newcombe said mournfully. "That company appealed the case, and we never got nothing. That really kind of finished Clara off. She just went downhill from then on. She never had any more seizures, but she always thought she was going to, and finally about two years ago she killed herself—stuck her head in the oven, turned the gas on, and by the time I found her, she was dead."

Newcombe paused, thought for a moment, and said, "After I went over the whole thing in my mind, I sued the company again, claiming the pills caused her to kill herself. But Questall had a whole bunch of attorneys and doctors to testify. There had been other cases where people who had taken the drug had had seizures similar to Clara's—so there was no doubt the pills were the cause —but none of the others committed suicide and none of those people sued. There couldn't have been many, because Questall pulled Resterin off the market so quickly that I think they'd discovered the effects it had almost as soon as we did. The judge threw my case out before there was a trial."

Mason asked, "Who were the witnesses for Questall?"

"At the first trial it was Jantzen, Benjamin Jantzen. That woman, Iris Jantzen, was their witness at the second hearing."

"I would imagine," Mason said, looking closely at Newcombe, "you didn't have much love for the company."

"No sir, I didn't."

"Or for Iris Jantzen."

"That would be a fair statement, too," Newcombe agreed.

"All right, Mr. Newcombe," Mason said, turning to leave. "I'm glad I heard your story. I'll still want you in court. I'll decide later whether or not to call you to testify."

"Yeah," Newcombe said. "I figured that's the way it would be."

Mason, Drake, and Sam Baylor went out into the rain.

The dog was still growling inside the house as Newcombe opened the screen door and left the porch.

Drake asked, "What do you think, Perry?"

"I think Mr. and Mrs. Newcombe got a bad deal from Questall Pharmaceuticals and Iris Jantzen."

Drake nodded.

Mason said, "I also think Bernard Newcombe would be a bad man to have for an enemy." He added, "Or for a friend, either, for that matter."

17

Court reconvened at 10:00 A.M. the next day.

D.A. Phillips announced his first witness.

"The People call Dr. Richard Shuler."

Mason, at the defense table, sat forward in his chair. Shuler was an expert DNA analyst. Mason knew he was there to testify about the blood found at the scene of the crime.

The doctor was in his mid-thirties, stocky in build, confident in manner, and had a thick crop of reddish hair and a bushy mustache the same color.

Phillips nodded to the doctor. "You tested the blood found in the sunroom where the victim, Iris Jantzen, was murdered, is that correct, Dr. Shuler?"

"That is correct. I did a DNA profile."

"Before you tell us your findings in this case, would

you explain to the court, for the record, the laboratory identification process known as DNA profiling?"

"Certainly," Dr. Shuler said. "DNA profiling was developed in Britain in the early 1980s. Basically, the process is predicated on the fact that DNA, or deoxyribonucleic acid, is contained in every cell in the human body. Different in each individual, DNA forms genes and carries the code for heredity. That being true, the root of a single hair, small skin samples, a spot of body fluids, or a bloodstain from an individual carries cells in which are contained that individual's unique DNA. Except for identical twins, every human being who has ever lived has a different DNA from every other human being who has ever lived. Am I making my explanation clear?"

Dr. Shuler looked at the judge and at the D.A.

Judge Maynard nodded. Phillips smiled and said, "Please proceed, Doctor."

Shuler said, "DNA profiling is performed by extracting the DNA from cells, contained, as I have previously stated, in hair, body fluids, skin samples, or bloodstains, and cutting it into smaller pieces. Then radioactive probes are added, and they combine with certain repetitive sequences of the four nucleotides that are DNA's building blocks. When the specimen is exposed to film over several days, a pattern results that is similar to grocery-store bar codes. Once we have that pattern established and recorded in a photograph, we compare it—a pattern established from a specimen left behind by an unknown individual—to an established pattern we have similarly created from a specimen from a known individual. When the two match, as can be seen by the eye, we have proven the existence of a genetic pattern that is unique to that one person out of many millions or even billions of others. DNA comparisons are similar to comparisons of human fingerprints, which we all understand. However, in criminal cases, one big advantage of DNA profiling is that biological evidence such as hair or skin or body fluids or blood is inadvertently left behind by criminals—and much more often discovered—than are fingerprints."

D.A. Phillips made a small bow toward the witness. "Thank you, Dr. Shuler. You've been most enlightening. Now, as to the DNA testing you did of the blood found at the scene of the murder of Iris Jantzen, would you tell the court what you found."

Dr. Shuler paused a moment to glance at a page of notes he had taken from his coat pocket.

"By a testing of blood found on the body of the victim, it was possible, through DNA profiling, to establish the victim's own blood as well as DNA from a second, unknown individual."

"And were you subsequently able to identify this second, unknown individual?"

"I was." Shuler nodded. "A comparison of DNA, from blood found on the victim's body, not the victim's, was positively identified as the DNA of John Leland when matched with DNA extracted from blood from John Leland that was recovered from a handkerchief he had used to wrap around a cut on his wrist, or arm."

Phillips produced a large chart and showed it to Shuler.

"Doctor, would you identify this chart?"

"It's a DNA profile comparison taken from the body of the victim and from John Leland."

"A perfect match," Phillips observed.

"A perfect match."

The D.A. asked that the chart be entered into evidence. He looked at Mason.

Mason had no objection.

Phillips turned back to the witness stand. "Earlier we have had evidence that a bloodstained gardener's glove was later found in the fireplace near the body of the victim. Did you do a DNA profile from the blood found on that glove?"

"I did."

"And what did you find?"

"That the DNA from the blood on the gardener's glove was the DNA of the victim, Iris Jantzen."

Again Phillips produced a chart. Dr. Shuler identified it as a DNA profile comparison taken from the gardener's glove and from the blood of Iris Jantzen. The D.A. asked that the chart be entered into evidence.

Mason had no objection.

Phillips turned toward the defense table. "Cross-examine," he said to Perry Mason.

Mason said, "The defense reserves the right to call this witness back at a later time."

Judge Maynard leaned forward. "Call your next witness, Mr. Phillips."

The D.A. said, "Your Honor, at this time we would like to present the videotaped testimony of Benjamin Jantzen. If the court will bear with us, it will take a few minutes to prepare for the showing of the tape."

"Very well, unless Mr. Mason has any objections," the judge said.

"No objections, Your Honor," Mason answered.

Judge Maynard rapped his gavel. "We will stand in recess for fifteen minutes."

While Phillips and a couple of the members of his staff began to move a large-screen television set to the front of the courtroom, Drake and Della Street joined Mason and John Leland at the defense table.

Leland, appearing pale and subdued, was glancing

around the courtroom. Mason suspected Leland wanted a look at Anne Kimbro.

Leland said, "I think I'll stretch my legs a bit."

Drake quickly stood. "Good idea. I'll join you."

Nice going, Paul, Mason thought, knowing Drake meant to keep an eye on Leland.

After they'd walked away, Della said, "How do you think it's going, Chief?"

"You wouldn't ask me that question, Della, unless you'd already guessed the answer." He half smiled. "Not good."

"You're right. That's what I guessed and was afraid of."

"Carter Phillips is putting together at the very least a prima facie case against our client," Mason admitted. "Sometime soon I have to find a way to blow it apart."

Della was frowning. "I wonder . . ."

She let the words trail off.

"Wonder what? Come on, Della. You know better than that. If you have something to say to me, say it."

"Well, have you ever considered that John Leland may not be telling you all he knows about the murder?"

Mason looked at her curiously. "What makes you ask that?"

"Call it a woman's intuition, maybe, but I know he's awfully smitten with Anne Kimbro. It makes me wonder if he'd ever reveal information that might put her in jeopardy."

Mason laughed and shook his head with admiration. "Oh, you have an intuition all right, Della. Yes, you do! The answer is that I have wondered the same thing. The problem is, what can I do about it? It's even occurred to me that he isn't half as worried about the predicament he's in as he is about losing her forever."

"Then you don't think he's told you everything he knows?"

"I don't think so, no," Mason said slowly. "But I don't think that whatever he's holding back, whether it's to protect Anne or not, will solve the murder. What I'm guessing is that whatever information he might be concealing would probably help his case but wouldn't clear him."

"But might also involve Anne," Della said quickly.

"That's my guess."

"But darn it, Perry, that makes your job harder. That's just not fair."

Mason shrugged philosophically.

The judge had returned to the bench. Carter Phillips had the TV set in place where it could be viewed by the spectators in the courtroom and by Judge Maynard. John Leland came back to the defense table and sat down.

Della started to slip away to join Drake in the first row of seats behind the defense table. Mason gave her a reassuring wink as she went.

In the front of the courtroom D.A. Phillips made a small speech. "The tape recording you are about to see was authorized by this court to take testimony pertinent to these proceedings from a witness, Benjamin Jantzen, who has been medically certified as being too ill to withstand the rigors of a personal appearance in court."

Phillips punched a button on the videocassette recorder attached to the TV set, and a scene appeared on the TV screen of the court clerk swearing in Benjamin Jantzen. Jantzen was in his mechanized wheelchair.

The court clerk stepped aside, and Carter Phillips appeared on screen with Jantzen.

Phillips asked, "Mr. Jantzen, do you know of any reason your deceased wife, Iris Jantzen, had for opposing the marriage of the defendant, John Leland, to your step-daughter, Anne Kimbro?"

The old man in the wheelchair nodded. "I do."

"And what was that reason?"

"She opposed the marriage because she believed John Leland was only interested in the money Anne will soon inherit."

"Iris Jantzen told you that?"

"She did."

"And do you know what she intended to do to make clear to John Leland her opposition to his marriage to Anne Kimbro?"

"I do. On the day of her murder, she went to the house in Coldwater Canyon to confront him with what she believed."

"How do you know that's what she was going to do?"

"She told me."

"She told you?"

"Yes, sir, she told me."

On the TV screen Carter Phillips looked directly into the camera and said, "No more questions."

He looked off-camera and added, "Your witness, Mr. Mason."

Phillips moved out of the picture, and Perry Mason appeared on screen with Benjamin Jantzen.

Mason nodded his head at Jantzen and said, "We've met before, Mr. Jantzen, you recall?"

Jantzen moved his wheelchair a couple of inches closer to Mason.

"Of course we have."

"And at the time we met, I asked you if your deceased wife, Iris Jantzen, told you why she was going to the house in Coldwater Canyon on that particular day. Do you remember that I asked you the question?"

"I remember. Yes."

"And do you remember your answer?"

"I didn't answer that question."

"Why didn't you answer the question?"

"Because," Jantzen said, a note of triumph in his voice, "I wanted to save my answer until I could give it in court!"

Mason shook his head wearily. "I have no further questions of this witness."

Mason consented with a show of indifference when Phillips asked that the videotape be entered into evidence.

While a couple of the D.A.'s assistants were removing the TV set, Carter Phillips called Anne Kimbro as his next witness, and she was sworn in by the court clerk.

It was apparent from Anne Kimbro's demeanor as she waited for the first question that she felt uncomfortable testifying in the proceedings. When Phillips moved in front of her, smiling reassuringly, she stared back at him with a wary, guarded expression.

"Miss Kimbro, we have already heard from the defendant's statement to the police of the purported events of the day of the murder that when you phoned him at the house in Coldwater Canyon, he told you Iris Jantzen was dead. Did he in fact tell you that?"

"Yes."

"Will you please tell the court what his exact words to you were."

Anne Kimbro paused to think before she answered.

"As I recall, he said, 'I just got here to the house and Iris was here and somebody has killed her.'"

Phillips repeated the words. "'I just got here to the house and Iris was here and somebody has killed her.' And then what did he say?"

"Actually, he didn't say anything for a few moments. And neither did I. I think we were both shocked, stunned."

"Or at least you were," the D.A. said quickly. "You can't really know what his feelings were, can you?"

Anne looked at Phillips, frowning.

He repeated the question.

She still didn't answer.

Judge Maynard admonished her gently, "Miss Kimbro, please answer the question."

Anne Kimbro paused to think before she answered.

"No," she said, "I guess I can't really *know* what his feelings were."

"When he did speak, what did Leland say next?"

"I asked him if he had notified the police. He said he had. Then I told him I thought he should have a lawyer present, and I phoned Mr. Perry Mason."

Phillips took a few paces up and down in front of the witness stand.

"You told him you thought he should have a lawyer, and he agreed, is that correct?"

"Yes."

"Why would you both think he'd need a lawyer, almost as soon as he told you that someone had killed Iris?"

"Because," she said reluctantly, "we both knew that because he and Iris didn't really get along, he'd be accused of killing her."

"And did you think he'd killed her?"

"Objection!" Mason said. "Immaterial! Calls for an opinion from the witness that she's no more qualified to answer than she would be qualified to know the defendant's feelings, as the prosecutor just pointed out."

"There's a certain logic to your objection, Mr. Mason, within the context of the prosecution's line of questioning," the judge said. "But I'm going to overrule."

Mason said, "The defense takes exception."

Judge Maynard nodded. "Let the record so note. The witness will answer the question."

Phillips asked quickly, "Did you think he'd killed her?"

"I—" Anne floundered briefly. "I truthfully don't know what I thought."

"Then you didn't think he hadn't killed her?"

"I just told you—"

"If you didn't know what you thought," Phillips said, "then you didn't think he hadn't killed her. That's my question."

"Truthfully—"

"Answer the question!"

Mason stood. "Objection, Your Honor! The prosecutor is badgering his own witness. She has tried to answer his question."

"I think I would agree," Judge Maynard said. "Let's move on, Mr. Phillips."

Phillips moved closer to the witness stand. "Miss Kimbro, the court has just heard testimony from your step-father on a videotape that Iris Jantzen went to the house where she met her death because she meant to confront Leland with her belief that he wanted to marry you because of your coming inheritance of a great deal of money. My question is, did you and Leland ever discuss your inheritance?"

She nodded. "The subject came up. It was one of a number of things we discussed during the time we knew one another. After all, we did plan to marry."

"Specifically," Phillips said, "wasn't there an occasion when John Leland suggested you should hire an auditor to go over the books of the company you were soon to inherit?" Phillips quickly added, "And didn't you mention this fact to a third party?"

"Obviously, you know the answer to the last question, Mr. Phillips. Yes, yes is the answer to both questions. John Leland was concerned about my best interests—"

"Furthermore," the D.A. interrupted, "didn't he, John Leland, actually go so far as to speak to someone he knew about auditing the books? Didn't he tell you he had someone to recommend?"

Phillips had turned away from the witness stand. During his last question to Anne Kimbro he, and most of the rest of the people present, were aware that a couple of men had entered the courtroom and conferred with Lieutenant Dallas, and the three had gathered with one of the D.A.'s assistants at the prosecution table. Now, Dallas was signaling frantically to Phillips.

Phillips turned to the judge. "Your Honor, the prosecution requests a brief moment to confer. There appears to be some matter of urgency requiring my presence at the prosecution table."

"This is a highly unusual request, Mr. Phillips." Judge Maynard was frowning. He looked at Mason. "Mr. Mason?"

Mason himself was curious about what was going on. "No objection, Your Honor."

"Your request is granted, Mr. Phillips," the judge said. "But be brief. The witness will remain on the stand."

Mason, along with everyone else, watched as Phillips, Lieutenant Dallas, and the two men huddled together.

Phillips turned and walked back toward the front of the courtroom. "Your Honor, may we approach the bench?" He made a sweeping motion with his arm to include Mason.

Judge Maynard said, "All right. Come forward, Mr. Phillips, Mr. Mason."

At the judge's bench, Phillips said, "Your Honor, I just received word that the fire marshals investigating the cause of the fire at the house where Iris Jantzen was murdered have called my office. They were delayed in their investigation yesterday because of the heavy rain. When they went to the scene today, they found that some-how, perhaps because of the rain, several stones had come loose and fallen from the stone fireplace, which was still standing. That's how they discovered the remains of a human skeleton that had been sealed up inside a section of the fireplace."

Phillips looked at the judge, then at Mason. "Under the circumstances, I think the court can appreciate the pressing need for the District Attorney's Office to inves-tigate the matter. Also, in fairness to the defendant in the present hearing, I think we should have certain facts es-tablished about the newly unearthed skeleton before we continue with these proceedings—even if, as is likely the case, the one circumstance may have no bearing upon the other. For these reasons I request a continuance of this hearing."

Judge Maynard looked at Mason.

Mason said quickly, "No objection. I concur that a continuance is in order."

"Since the weekend is coming up," the judge said, "I will grant a continuance for five days, until next Tuesday."

Judge Maynard made his announcement of a contin-uance to the packed courtroom, told Anne Kimbro that she was excused for the day, reminded her that she would take the witness stand again when the hearing resumed, and adjourned.

Newsmen present were dashing around the room, trying, without success, to find out the reason for the continuance. D.A. Phillips pushed his way past them. Lieutenant Ray Dallas had left the courtroom. Mason hurried back to the defense table.

"What's going on, Perry?" Drake asked.

Mason took Drake to one side. "I want you to get one of your men to babysit John Leland until Tuesday."

"Baylor's outside, standing by in case I need him."

"Get him," Mason said. "Then I want you to go with me."

Drake hurried away.

"Della," Mason said, turning, "gather up my notes, please. Then I want you to take them back to the office. I'll be in touch with you."

"Right, Chief."

John Leland, who had been hovering in the background, came forward. "What's happening, Mr. Mason?"

Mason took Leland by the arm. "There's no time to talk now, John. Something's come up. I'll fill you in on all the details as soon as I know them. But for now, and this is very important, I want you to go home and stay there until I contact you. One of Drake's men, Sam Baylor, is going with you. I want him there with you until I tell you otherwise. Do you have that straight?"

"Yes, sir."

"Good. Here's Baylor now," Mason said, as Drake returned with the operative.

Mason watched Leland and Baylor leave.

Then he said to Drake, "Come on, Paul, let's go."

"Where are we going?"

"Out to the house where Iris Jantzen was murdered. The fire marshals just notified the D.A. and Dallas that they've uncovered a skeleton that was sealed up in the fireplace of the house."

Drake gave a low, sharp whistle.

Mason grinned. "I couldn't have expressed it better myself, Paul."

18

The area of burnt-out rubble where the house had stood was still enclosed by the police yellow tape that had printed on it the warning CRIME SCENE. DO NOT ENTER.

Mason and Drake stood outside the barrier, waiting until the fire marshals, the police, the medical examiner, and D.A. Phillips finished their inspection of the skeleton and the section of the fireplace where the skeleton had been found. Long hoses attached to pumping machines snaked across the grounds, emptying out the water that had collected from the previous day's rain on the rubble.

"Man, it looks like a bomb hit," Drake said.

"One sure thing about it," Mason observed. "There won't be any more murders committed in that house."

"You think somebody wanted to make certain of that?" Drake asked.

Mason nodded. "It could have been." He recalled Anne

Kimbro's words that she almost believed the house had a curse on it, and that she no longer ever wanted to live in it.

Behind the barrier the driver of the waiting morgue van and an assistant placed the skeleton in a body bag, loaded it inside the van, and drove away. The medical examiner, D.A. Phillips, and most of the police and fire marshals left. Lieutenant Dallas had remained, poking around the section of the stone fireplace where the body had been concealed.

Mason ducked under the yellow tape, saying, "Wait for me, Paul."

Dallas glanced up as Mason approached him. Dallas said, "I thought you'd turn up."

"You should have known that you could count on it," Mason answered. "What'd you find, Ray?"

Dallas turned his hand in the air. "No reason why you shouldn't know, I guess. The medical examiner couldn't tell much yet about the skeleton we found. Apparently, the body had been wrapped in some kind of encasement—plastic or rubber—and the M.E. does believe some substance, probably lime, he said, was put in with the body at the time it was sealed up. From what's left of the clothes it would appear it's the skeleton of a male."

Dallas looked off into the distance, then back at Mason. "There was a gun in with the body, too. A thirty-eight revolver. Two bullets have been fired from it. We found one of the spent bullets in with the skeleton."

"Refresh my memory, Ray. What caliber gun was used to kill Elizabeth Jantzen?"

"A thirty-eight."

"So now we can assume we know where Edward Larner disappeared to after the murder of Elizabeth Jantzen."

Dallas rubbed his chin. "That's a premature assumption. But likely. We'll know more when Forensic gets through with its examination of the skeleton."

"How did the marshals come to spot it sealed into the fireplace?"

Dallas pointed. "A couple of the large stones there had fallen out, and one of the marshals noticed what looked like a piece of bone back in there. They started to dig in, and that's when they uncovered the whole skeleton."

Mason bent and peered inside the fireplace. He could see the chiseled-out recess behind the stone front. Pieces of the concrete that had been used to seal in the body had been chipped away by the marshals and lay at the bottom of the fireplace.

"It was a pretty amateurish job," Dallas observed. "Whoever hid the body in there just slapped the concrete over it to conceal it."

Dallas frowned. "Funny thing about the stones that came loose; the fire marshals speculate that the rain could have caused it to happen. But they haven't ruled out the possibility that somebody could have been here since the fire and deliberately prized them out so the skeleton would be found. If that was the case, I'd sure like to know why."

"So would I," Mason said thoughtfully. "So would I."

One of the detectives who had accompanied Dallas to the scene had walked back to where their unmarked car was parked. The detective called out to Dallas, "Lieutenant, the dispatcher's trying to raise you on the radio."

"Yeah, coming," Dallas yelled back. He ducked under the yellow tape barrier and headed for the car.

Mason followed, stopping to speak with Drake.

"What gives, Perry?"

"They've got a skeleton, probably male, they think, from what's left of the clothes he was wearing, a thirty-eight revolver and a spent thirty-eight bullet, all of which had been wrapped in plastic or rubber and sealed up in concrete inside the fireplace."

"*Edward Larner!*" Drake exclaimed.

Before Mason could answer, Dallas was calling to him.

Mason went to the unmarked car.

Dallas said, "A report just came in. Police were called to the Jantzen house and found Benjamin Jantzen dead. He was slumped over in the front seat of a car in the garage. The garage was filled with carbon-monoxide fumes. Guess who called the police to the house?" Dallas paused to give his next words more weight: "Your client. John Leland."

Mason's answer was a mixture of bafflement and exasperation. "I don't see how that could be. Are you sure there hasn't been a mistake?"

The answer Dallas gave seemed to eliminate that possibility: "The police there report that Leland won't answer any questions unless you, his lawyer, are present."

Dallas, with a wave of his hand, started up the car and drove away.

Mason turned and looked at Drake, who had been standing behind him, listening to the exchange between Mason and Dallas.

Drake said quickly, "I know what you're wondering, Perry. All I can tell you is that Sam Baylor's one of my best men. If Leland gave him the slip and went out to the Jantzen house, then Leland's had to pull off a trick worthy of—what was his first name, Harry?—Houdini."

19

"Look, Mr. Mason," John Leland said earnestly, "the explanation is very simple, if you'll just consider things from my point of view."

Mason and Leland were sitting in the study in the Jantzen house. Dallas and the other police had left them alone there when Mason said he wanted a word in private with his client. Through the window of the study Mason could see the police checking the garage where Benjamin Jantzen's body still remained, awaiting the arrival of the medical examiner.

Mason leaned forward toward Leland. "Explain," he said grimly. "It sure as hell would be helpful to have some simple explanation, for a change."

Leland swallowed hard. "After we left the courthouse today, I got to thinking about Anne's testimony on the witness stand. How she tried not to say anything that would be damaging to me. How she was trying to protect me and still answer truthfully all the questions being thrown at her by the D.A." He looked at Mason pleadingly. "You saw that in court, didn't you? You knew she was trying to help me, didn't you? Didn't you think that?"

"Forget what I think. Let me hear this simple explanation of how you gave Sam Baylor the slip and why you came out here today."

"I'm trying to tell you. I was thinking all this about Anne after Sam Baylor and I went back to my apartment. I wanted Anne to know how much it meant to me, what she was trying to do. I wanted to tell her. That's all. I knew I couldn't do it with Baylor right on top of me all the time. When we were in the apartment, I told him I wanted to take a shower. I figured he wouldn't follow me in there. So I went in the bathroom, turned on the shower, climbed out the bathroom window, got in my car, and left. I stopped at the first phone booth I got to, and called the house here. Neal answered. You know, Neal Granin, Iris's brother. Neal said Anne wasn't home yet. Neal and I have always been good friends. He suggested I come out to the house and talk to Anne. He said he had to run an errand, but that he'd probably be back by the time I got there. He thought Anne would be there, too."

"So, of course you came right out here," Mason said. "Let's hear what happened then."

Leland said, "I got here, and I didn't find anyone home. The servants were away on errands. Neal hadn't gotten back, and Anne wasn't here, either. I figured Mr. Jantzen was with one or the other of them. So I wandered around outside, and then I thought I heard the sound of a motor running. I thought it was coming from inside the garage. I went to look. It was the motor of a car inside the garage, all right. The garage door was closed. I opened it, and the place was full of fumes. Mr. Jantzen's wheelchair was lying on its side near the front door of the car. I put a handkerchief over my face, went to the car, saw Mr. Jantzen inside, and turned off the engine. I saw that Mr. Jantzen was dead. I couldn't find his heart beating. I had to drive to a phone booth to call the police. Afterward, I came back here. Neal got here just a few minutes before the police did. Anne came home a little after that."

Mason was curious. "Did you talk to Anne?"

"No. The police were here by then. I didn't talk to anyone after the police got here. Before, Neal and I talked briefly. I had to be the one to tell him about Mr. Jantzen."

"What was his reaction?"

"He was shocked at first, I think. But then he kept trying to reassure me—"

"Reassure you about what?"

"Well, by then I had begun to realize that the police might get to wondering if *I* had had anything to do with Mr. Jantzen's death. I mean, it suddenly occurred to me that here I was the one who'd discovered his body and called the police, just the way it had happened with Iris. That's why I told the police I wouldn't talk until you were present, the way you instructed me the other time."

"That's about the only thing you seem to have remembered that I instructed you to do," said Mason, his voice hard. "Now, tell me what Neal Granin said to reassure you about what the police might think."

Leland nodded. "He said it was obvious that Mr. Jantzen must have committed suicide. He said it was obvious that Mr. Jantzen had gone out to the garage in his wheelchair, shut the garage doors behind him, climbed into the car from the wheelchair—all of which Neal said Mr. Jantzen was capable of doing—and committed suicide. He said the police would have to see that."

"Did he tell you he knew of any reason why Jantzen might have killed himself?"

"What he said was that Mr. Jantzen seemed depressed in recent days. He said he thought Iris's death had been more than Mr. Jantzen could handle. He told me that Mr. Jantzen had been despondent since his most recent stroke of a few months ago, anyway."

"Did either of you discuss Anne after you got here and Neal came back?"

"No. That's all we talked about, what I told you."

"So you don't know where Anne was?"

"No."

Lieutenant Dallas opened the door to the study and came in.

"We need a statement from you," Dallas said, pointing to Leland.

"Okay, Lieutenant," Mason said. "Mr. Leland's agreeable."

Dallas pulled over a chair, turned it backward, and sat down, resting his arms on the top of the chair. "Tell me about it, Mr. Leland."

Leland went through the story he'd told Mason.

When he'd finished, all Dallas said was, "I'll need a signed statement from you."

"We'll oblige," Mason said.

One of the detectives from headquarters entered the study.

Mason said to Leland, "You go with this officer, John. Wait for me outside. I want a word with the lieutenant."

Leland and the detective left the room.

Mason looked at Dallas. "I'm not going to ask you what you think, Ray. What happened here today will sort itself out, in time. If you find out what I think you're going to find out about that skeleton you have at the lab, I have a suggestion for you."

Dallas's eyes narrowed. "Is this some kind of a diversion you've dreamed up to shift suspicion away from your client?"

"I told you," Mason said patiently, "my suggestion has to do with the first Jantzen murder, the murder of Elizabeth Jantzen, and the skeleton."

"All right, what?"

"Did you ever take a look at the copies of those anonymous hate letters the Jantzen family, especially Iris, received?"

"I saw them, yeah. I figured they were just crank letters."

"Maybe," Mason said. "I had a talk with Bernard Newcombe, the guy who sued the Jantzens and Questall Pharmaceuticals twice—and lost both times."

"I know who he is," Dallas said. "His wife took some medication made by the company and died, or something. You think he wrote the anonymous letters, is that it? So what if he did?"

Mason nodded. "I think he did. But that's not what interests me. I have a hunch that to put some of the pieces together in the Larner-Jantzen case, you might want to take a look at Clara Newcombe's medical records, which must have been part of the evidence when Newcombe brought suit. Then I think you ought to dig out whatever medical information the police collected on Benjamin Jantzen at the time of Elizabeth Jantzen's murder."

Dallas frowned. "Do you know something you're not telling me?"

"No, I don't, Ray. This is just a hunch I have that may prove helpful to you if, as I said, you find out what I think you're going to find out about the skeleton."

Dallas said, "I'll look into it. But I'll admit that I'm curious as to how anything we turn up about the murder of Elizabeth Jantzen can be of benefit to your client."

"Did I say it would? Can't you just assume that, as a good citizen, I'd want to do whatever I could to see that murder solved?"

"Sure you would, Counselor. The only problem is, I know you. When you're in the middle of a murder trial, as you are now, all your energies go into the defense of your client. It's not like you to be interested in other matters, like an ancient murder case."

"Whatever you think," Mason said, "can I count on you to let me know if there was anything to my hunch?"

"You can count on it," Dallas assured him.

Mason grinned. "I like to know I've done my civic duty, Lieutenant."

20

On Tuesday morning, an hour before the 10 A.M. time set for the continuance of John Leland's preliminary hearing, Perry Mason sat facing Ray Dallas in the lieutenant's office at police headquarters. Dallas had phoned Mason earlier, and Mason had come directly from his apartment to the meeting.

"I thought you should know what we now know about most of the circumstances of Elizabeth Jantzen's murder," Dallas said.

Mason nodded.

"The skeleton was Edward Larner's. Forensic verified the fact beyond a doubt from copies of old dental X rays of Larner along with a lot of other data. From their examination of the skeleton they determined he was killed by the thirty-eight bullet found with the skeleton, and that the gun found with the skeleton was used to fire the thirty-eight bullet. They also matched the bullet that killed Elizabeth Jantzen to that same thirty-eight revolver."

Dallas looked pleased as he rocked back in his swivel chair. "Furthermore, Forensic tied the thirty-eight revolver directly to Benjamin Jantzen. Know how? Fingerprints, Jantzen's, on the gun. Would you believe it? The body, the bullet, and the gun all stashed away inside the fireplace. And he didn't think to wipe his fingerprints away."

"It happens," Mason said

"Oh, and another thing," Dallas said, "your hunch about the medical reports on Newcombe's wife, Clara, and Jantzen's medical reports at the time of the murder, was helpful in tying up a loose end, if I understand correctly what your hunch was."

Mason smiled. "That Jantzen knew because of the lawsuit brought before the murder that the medication Resterin, made by Questall, could induce symptoms that mimicked a stroke. So as soon as he killed Elizabeth, after he must have followed her to her meeting with Larner, and killed Larner, he took the medication, had what appeared to be a stroke—as verified by the doctors—and avoided being interrogated by the police."

"It appears it had to have been that way," Dallas agreed. "According to the time element on the day of those murders, Jantzen had his stroke, or what was diagnosed as a stroke, almost simultaneously with the killings. His medical reports then were identical to those of Clara Newcombe. In recent years, again according to medical reports, the strokes he had were real."

"And now years later," Mason interjected, "when Jantzen knew that Larner's skeleton would be discovered sooner or later after the house burned down, Benjamin Jantzen committed suicide in the car in the garage."

"Yeah, well." Dallas paused, looking uncomfortable. "There is one hitch about Jantzen's suicide."

"What's that?"

Dallas made a brushing-aside motion with his hand. "It's not important, just peculiar. The autopsy on Jantzen, according to the medical examiner, showed a level of less than fifteen percent CO—the chemical term for carbon monoxide—in the body. Less than fifteen percent is not sufficient to cause death."

Mason frowned. "Then what was the cause of death?"

"That's a gray area; you can take your pick. Officially, the autopsy report lists hardening of the arteries, the result of which is that the heart stopped beating."

Mason was astonished. "Here's a guy in a car in a closed garage, the car's motor is running, the garage is full of carbon-monoxide fumes, and we're told the victim died of hardening of the arteries!"

"I know, I know," Dallas said quickly. "I pressed the M.E. pretty hard on the point myself. I still think Leland had something to do with Jantzen's death, but the M.E. wouldn't budge from his official finding."

Mason shook his head. "It makes no sense; not that I think Leland killed him." He looked at Dallas shrewdly. "You said I could take my pick of what caused his death. What's the other possibility?"

"Jantzen could have been smothered, suffocated, so I'm told. For instance, a pillow could have been placed over his face, cutting off his air supply. Perhaps while he slept, or was taken by surprise. But unless there's evidence on the body that that's what happened, marks, bruises, contusions on the face or neck—and there were none on Jantzen's body—there's no medical method of distinguishing between a death brought on by smothering or suffocation and hardening of the arteries, both of which similarly result in the heart stopping. The medical examiner and his staff say they have no alternative except to stand by their official finding."

Dallas stood up. "Carter Phillips wanted you to know what we know before Leland's hearing resumes this morning."

Mason stood, too. "Okay, Ray, now I know."

"Look at it this way," Dallas said. "At least now we know what happened in the Larner-Jantzen case, and, what's just as important, that there was no connection between the murder of Elizabeth Jantzen and Iris Jantzen."

Mason said nothing. He gave Dallas a wave of his hand and left the office, then walked the short distance to the courthouse, concentrating his thoughts on how to prove what he now believed to be the solution to the murder of Iris Jantzen.

At the courthouse Mason had to push through the crowds in the corridor who had come to attend the hearing and couldn't get inside the courtroom, where every seat was taken.

Della Street and Drake were in their usual seats. John Leland was sitting at the defense table, looking anxious, until Mason came in.

When Judge Maynard appeared, he called Carter Phillips and Mason to the bench.

"I assume both you gentlemen are familiar with the full report on the skeleton found at the house where the two women, Elizabeth Jantzen and later Iris Jantzen, met their deaths, as well as the death of Benjamin Jantzen?" the judge asked.

Both men answered affirmatively.

"Do either of you see any reason why this hearing should not continue?"

"No, none," the D.A. answered.

Mason shook his head. "No, Your Honor."

Judge Maynard reconvened the court and called Anne Kimbro back to the stand to continue her examination by Carter Phillips. The judge reminded Anne Kimbro that she was still under oath.

The D.A. stood briefly in front of the witness stand, glancing at the notes he held in his hand before he said, "Miss Kimbro, at the time this court adjourned on Wednesday of last week, you were testifying to certain discussions you and the defendant had had concerning your inheritance, you remember?"

"Yes, I do."

Phillips nodded. "I had asked you if John Leland had told you he had someone to recommend to you to do an audit on the books of the company you were soon to inherit. Court adjourned before you were able to answer. Would you now answer the question, please."

"Yes. He did mention to me that he knew of an auditor who could go over the books of Questall Pharmaceuticals."

"Did John Leland mention to you why he thought there should be an audit?"

"No."

"So," Phillips said, "the fact is that he was interested in your inheritance, just as Benjamin Jantzen testified was the belief of Iris Jantzen."

"As I stated earlier, Mr. Phillips, John and I planned to be married; we discussed many aspects of our lives."

"Did you tell Iris about John Leland's suggestion that the company books should be audited?"

Anne shook her head. "No. I did mention it, in passing, to Neal, Neal Granin. He may have told her. I didn't."

Phillips took a couple of paces away, turned, and came back to the front of the witness stand. "Now, you have just testified that you and Leland discussed many aspects of your lives."

"Yes."

"But he didn't tell you his true identity, did he?"

"No."

"And when you found out who he really was, how did you feel about him?"

Anne bit her lower lip. "I was—well, I guess, numb. I don't know what I felt."

"Surely, deceived, at the least?"

"I have never had time to think it all through, to find out what my true feelings are about that."

"If you had known his true identity at the time you talked to him on the phone and he told you Iris Jantzen had been murdered, would you still have thought he should have a lawyer present?"

"Objection!" Mason interjected. "Calls for speculation on the part of the witness."

Judge Maynard nodded. "Sustained."

"No further questions," Phillips said.

Mason stayed seated at the defense table as he asked the first question of his cross-examination.

"You have said in your statement to the police that on the day of the murder you phoned John Leland at the house in Coldwater Canyon and learned of the death of Iris Jantzen. Is that correct?"

Anne was frowning. "Yes."

"In his statement to the police, John Leland says he phoned you at your house, and there was no answer. Yet almost directly after that, you called him."

"I did phone him, yes."

"My question is, where were you when you phoned him?"

"I was in my car. I phoned him from my car."

"From your car," Mason repeated musingly. "I don't recall that you mentioned that fact previously. Do you recall that you did?"

Anne shook her head. "I—I can't recall, one way or the other."

"I was under the impression that you were home at the time you phoned him," Mason said thoughtfully. "At any rate, now we know you were in your car. And since we know that, I'm curious why you didn't drive directly to the house, the house where John Leland was. Where did you go after you talked on the phone to him?"

"I . . . drove home. Then I went back out to the canyon. As you know. You were there."

Mason got up slowly. "Why would you go home?"

"I guess," Anne said haltingly, "I just did it out of reflex; I had been headed home when I phoned John, and I simply continued on."

Mason had walked forward to the witness box. "Exactly where had you been when you were in your car and phoned Leland?"

"I had been out, doing an errand for Iris. Actually, as you've heard from him, I was supposed to be at the house before he was, but I was delayed. That was why I had had to call John earlier at his office and tell him I'd be late meeting him."

"What was the errand?"

"Neal phoned me from the office. He said Iris had asked him to call me. She had told him she had an important meeting to attend, and she'd be late getting home. She'd ordered a cake from the bakery we use, and since she was going to be late, she wanted me to pick up the cake."

"This bakery, how far is it from your house?" Mason asked.

"About a mile." Anne raised a hand when she saw that Mason was about to ask another question. She said, "But I have to explain. When I got to the bakery, the cake wasn't ready."

"So you waited."

"No. I drove around for a while."

"For quite a long while," Mason suggested, "if I've been able to correctly calculate the time that elapsed from when you must have visited the bakery for the first time until you phoned John Leland."

"Well, yes, I guess it was. I wanted to give the bakery plenty of time before I went back."

"So you drove around?"

"Yes."

"Did anyone see you while you were driving, anyone you might know, anyone who might be able to say he'd seen you?"

"Objection, Your Honor." Phillips was gesturing urgently. "Counsel's questions are improper. This witness is not on trial."

Judge Maynard had been following Anne's testimony closely. He looked from her to Phillips to Mason and back at Anne, and said, "Overruled, Mr. Phillips. The witness will answer the question."

"I can't think of anyone who might have seen me," she said hesitantly.

Mason nodded. "So we have quite a period of time when your whereabouts cannot be confirmed."

Phillips was gesturing again. "Objection!"

"Sustained."

"Turning to another matter," Mason said, smiling slightly, "are you familiar with John Leland's statement to the police that on the day he first went to the house in Coldwater Canyon and met you, he had received a phone call directing him to that particular address?"

Anne nodded. "Yes."

"Do you have any idea who might have made that call, and so lured him to the house?"

"Objection! Objection, Your Honor!" Phillips was red-faced. "The prosecution has been unable to verify the defendant's unsubstantiated claim that such a phone call was ever received at his office."

"I'll sustain," the judge ruled. "Mr. Mason, I think your present line of questioning of this witness has reached its end."

"Yes, Your Honor," Mason said agreeably. "I have no further questions."

Judge Maynard looked at Phillips. The prosecutor shook his head.

The judge said, "The witness is excused." He banged his gavel. "The court will take a fifteen-minute recess."

21

Perry Mason used the time during the brief recess of the hearing to inform John Leland of the facts he had learned from Lieutenant Dallas earlier about the identity of the skeleton found in the fireplace and of the death of Benjamin Jantzen. It was the first chance Mason had had to talk to Leland that morning about the two developments.

"So my father didn't kill Elizabeth Jantzen, after all," Leland said wonderingly. "And all these years I thought . . ." He shook his head. Then he asked, "Does Anne know?"

Mason glanced toward the back of the courtroom, where he saw Carter Phillips and Ray Dallas talking to Anne. Neal Granin had accompanied her to court that day, since Granin was scheduled to testify next in the hearing.

"I think she's being told now," Mason said, directing

Leland's attention to where Anne was sitting with Phillips, Dallas, and Granin.

Leland said, "I have to have some time to think before I can understand all that's happening."

"Don't try to understand it now. I want you to concentrate on the hearing. I want you to listen carefully to all the prosecution's testimony. If you hear or have heard anyone say anything that's not true, you must tell me. I need to know."

"You're really asking me about the testimony Anne just gave, aren't you?" Leland looked at Mason probingly. "You were pretty rough with her."

"Never mind how rough I was. What about her testimony?"

"Truthfully," Leland said slowly, "I never knew she was in her car when she phoned me the day Iris was murdered."

"If you had known, you would have expected her to drive directly out to where you were, isn't that so?"

"I guess I would. But do you think it's that important? I mean, she was shocked when I told her what had happened. She probably wasn't thinking straight."

Mason said, "I don't know whether it's important or not. What we're trying to do here is get as many facts as we can out into the open. Then we put those facts together and see what they add up to."

Leland was frowning. "I'll tell you something I never considered before, either; that Anne might have been the one who phoned my office that first time and got me out to that house. I was dumbfounded when you asked her if she knew who had made that phone call."

"You shouldn't have been," Mason said brusquely. "You said there was such a phone call, even though you can't prove it. Which leaves me with the choice of either believing you or not. If I believe you, then I have to try to find out who called you."

Judge Maynard returned to the bench, and the bailiff announced that the hearing was again in session.

Carter Phillips stepped to the front of the courtroom and called Neal Granin as the next witness.

The D.A.'s first question was, "Iris Jantzen, the victim, was your sister?"

"Yes."

"And you lived with her and Benjamin Jantzen and Anne Kimbro from the time your sister married Mr. Jantzen?"

"I did. I have."

"And you worked for the Jantzen company, Questall Pharmaceuticals, is that correct?"

"Yes, sir."

"You were a part of the family?"

"Yes, sir."

"When you first met the defendant, John Leland, what were your feelings about him?"

Granin smiled. "I liked him. John and I have always been good friends."

"And did your sister, Iris, like him?"

"As far as I could tell, everyone in the family liked John."

"In the beginning?" Phillips asked.

"Yes. I think we all wanted Anne to be happy, and since John made her happy, well, we liked him."

"But that was just in the beginning, wasn't it?"

"No. Not just in the beginning. I've always liked—"

Phillips interrupted, "I'm not referring to *your* feelings now. I'm referring to your sister's feelings about him.

Didn't her feelings change somewhere along the line, and weren't you, weren't the others, even John Leland himself, aware of the change?"

"I suppose, yes."

"No." Phillips shook his head. "It was more than 'suppose.' In fact, you knew, and so did everyone else know, that Iris was opposed to the marriage of John Leland and Anne Kimbro. Isn't that so?"

Neal Granin's answer came slowly. "Her feelings did change, and yes, I think we all realized it. She never said anything directly, but she did want Anne and John to delay the date of the wedding."

"Didn't her feelings, which had become apparent, ever concern you? Didn't you ever ask her about them?"

Granin shook his head. "Speaking for myself, I believed Iris would come around eventually and accept John. I thought the others, particularly Anne, felt that way, too."

"And what about John Leland? Do you think he felt that way? Or was he, more likely, deeply troubled by the opposition of Iris?"

Granin hunched his shoulders. "I can't really say. If he was, in your words 'deeply troubled,' he did a good job of concealing it. I'd say he even went out of his way to try to please Iris, to be friends with her."

Phillips folded his arms. "Now, let's get to the reason Benjamin Jantzen gave as to why Iris didn't like John Leland; that she felt he was only interested in Anne's inheritance. Did you know that was her reason?"

"Did I know?"

"Yes, did you know? Did you ever hear her say that was her reason for her feelings about the defendant?"

"I suppose," Granin answered slowly, "I heard her mention it some time or other, in an offhand way."

Phillips moved in closer to the witness stand. "So, when you heard Benjamin Jantzen testify on videotape that Iris went to confront John Leland with her feelings on the day of her murder, you weren't surprised, were you?"

Granin was silent.

Judge Maynard said, "The witness will answer the question."

"No," Granin said.

Phillips said, "I have no further questions."

Neal Granin turned in his chair as Perry Mason came toward him.

"Mr. Granin, I would like us to review the afternoon of the day Iris Jantzen was murdered. We have had testimony from Anne Kimbro that you phoned her at home and told her that Iris had an important meeting to attend and that Iris wanted Anne to pick up a cake for her, is that correct?"

"Yes, it is. I did call Anne after Iris asked me to do so."

"Did Iris tell you, in fact, that she was going to see John Leland?"

Granin shook his head. "No, she did not."

"Iris didn't tell you she was going to see John Leland, and you, in turn, didn't tell Anne that Iris was going to the house in Coldwater Canyon?"

"No. I couldn't have told Anne that; Iris didn't tell me."

Mason nodded. "Is it possible then that Iris herself might have called Anne and told her?"

"I—I don't see why she would have."

Mason persisted. "But you don't know that she didn't. I gather that after Iris told you she had an important meeting to attend and then went to the house to see John Leland, you didn't know where she was or what she might have done?"

"I guess I didn't know."

"Didn't know whether or not Iris herself called Anne?"

"No, I didn't know, I don't know. But I don't see why—"

"Your Honor!" Mason looked up at the bench.

Judge Maynard said, "Mr. Granin, you will confine your answers to the question counsel asks."

Granin nodded. "Yes, sir."

Mason said, "You have just testified to the prosecutor about how John Leland reacted to Iris when it became clear that her feelings toward him changed. How about Anne's attitude toward Iris on the matter? Was she deeply troubled?"

"I think Anne felt as I did; that eventually Iris would accept John."

"And do you think," Mason asked, "Anne would ever believe John Leland was only interested in her because of her inheritance, no matter what Iris said or tried to do?"

"No," Granin said emphatically, "I don't think Anne would ever believe that of John. She loved him. Totally."

"Thank you," Mason said. "No further questions."

Judge Maynard looked toward the prosecution table. "Mr. Phillips, do you have any questions on redirect?"

"No, Your Honor," the D.A. said. "The People rest."

"Mr. Mason"—the judge sat forward at the bench— "we're approaching the lunch hour, and I have court business elsewhere this afternoon. I would like to conclude these proceedings as soon as possible without putting undue pressure on you. Would you like to call your first defense witness in the time remaining this morning, or wait until court reconvenes tomorrow?"

"Actually, Your Honor," Mason said, "I reserved the right to call one of the prosecution's witnesses at a later time, if the court recalls. The witness was Dr. Richard

Shuler. I would like to call Dr. Shuler now, dispose of my cross-examination, and open my defense rebuttal tomorrow."

Judge Maynard said, "Proceed."

Dr. Shuler, the DNA expert, took the witness stand.

"Dr. Shuler," Mason said, "you have testified that through DNA testing, you were able to determine that the defendant's blood was found on the body of the victim and that the victim's blood was found on the gardener's glove, is that correct?"

"Yes, that is correct."

"But you found no trace of the victim's blood on John Leland's handkerchief?"

"No, I did not."

"And you found no trace of John Leland's blood on the gardener's glove?"

"No."

"To your knowledge, was blood found elsewhere in the sunroom?"

"Not to my knowledge, no. I assume that if it had, I would have been given samples to test."

"I see." Mason was frowning. "I believe you testifed that you are able to extract DNA from cells not only contained in bloodstains but from cells in hair, body fluids, or skin samples. Is that correct?"

"Yes." Dr. Shuler smiled. "I did testify to that, and it is true."

"And did you, in fact, do tests on any hair, body fluids, or skin samples recovered from the scene of the murder?"

"I did not. I do not know that any such samples were recovered."

"I'm curious, Doctor. If such samples were collected, could you still do DNA testing on them, even if there had been a passage of time since they were left at the scene?

For example, if—say—a hair was found, and it had been there for a period of time and would have, I would think, dried out, could you still do a DNA analysis on it?"

Dr. Shuler nodded his head. "In the case of a hair, years could pass, ten, twenty, twenty-five years or so, and as long as the root was attached, a DNA analysis would still be possible. We would use a process called Dot Blot, in which the dried-out hair would be rehydrated, making possible a DNA analysis."

"If, for example," Mason said, "the house in Coldwater Canyon had not been destroyed by fire, as it was, it would be possible to recover and analyze such samples—which might have been overlooked—from the scene even now?"

"Absolutely."

"Does it not seem strange to you, Doctor, that there were no specimens recovered from the sunroom other than the bloodstains you were given to analyze?"

"Objection!" Carter Phillips protested, standing. "This witness was not a part of the forensic team that gathered evidence at the time of the murder. He has no knowledge that would enable him to answer counsel's question."

"Sustained."

Mason smiled. "I have two final questions, Dr. Shuler. We have heard testimony from you that the gardener's glove on which you identified the victim's blood was a left-handed glove, is that not true?"

"Yes. It was a left-handed glove."

Mason took a couple of paces away from the witness stand and turned back. "My final question is, were you also given that glove's mate, the right-handed gardener's glove, to examine, as well?"

Dr. Shuler paused for a moment before he said, "No, I was not given the right-handed gardener's glove to examine."

"Thank you, Doctor. No more questions."

Judge Maynard looked at Carter Phillips.

The D.A. appeared puzzled. He said, "No questions."

"This hearing is adjourned until tomorrow at ten A.M." The judge hurried away and disappeared through the door to his chambers.

Mason, at the defense table, said to John Leland, "I'm sending you home again with Drake's investigator, Sam Baylor, and this time I want you to stay there."

Leland said, "This time you have my word I will."

Mason turned to Drake, who was waiting nearby. "Everything in place, Paul?"

Drake nodded.

"Okay," Mason said. "You go ahead. I'll join you as soon as I'm finished here."

Della Street had gathered Mason's notes together and had put them into his briefcase. She took the briefcase, and she and Drake walked away as Lieutenant Dallas strolled toward Mason.

"Talk to you a minute, Counselor?" Dallas asked.

"Sure, Ray. What's on your mind?"

"Your last round of questions kind of shook Phillips up. He suspects you're going to try to pull one of your famous surprises."

Dallas looked at Mason warily. "I confess I didn't get the point of them, either. All that stuff about evidence that might have been recovered if the house hadn't burned down. If you'll take my word for it, I can assure you that the forensic team swept that sunroom clean. There was nothing there that was overlooked."

Mason shrugged. "If you say so."

"So, what frankly puzzles me is the point of your cross-examination of Dr. Shuler."

"Let's say," Mason said, "I was baiting the hook so you

can catch the real murderer of Iris Jantzen. That is, if you'll trust me enough to follow my suggestions and believe that the defense wants no particular credit if what I have in mind solves this murder. The homicide squad will get all the honors."

Dallas stuck out his hand. "You have a deal."

22

Lieutenant Ray Dallas said, "Perry, I have to confess that I'm beginning to wonder if this waiting around until the possible killer appears is going to pay off. It looks to me like all we're going to leave here with is a lot of bug bites and cramped muscles."

Mason and Ray Dallas were hidden in the trees and bushes around the clearing in Coldwater Canyon where Anne Kimbro's house had once stood. Ordinarily, Mason wouldn't have come on a stakeout such as this, but his chief hope of clearing John Leland depended upon what happened out here, and he wanted to be present.

The grounds of the clearing were still covered with black ash from the fire. The smoke-blackened stone chimney, lighted from behind by the sun setting behind the trees to the west, was like a dark shadow casting a second dark shadow across the ground.

Other members of the LAPD were concealed in the trees. The positions they had taken formed a circle around the clearing. Also, two giant searchlights had been brought in, and were hidden out of sight in the surrounding woods. All of the men were equipped with walkie-talkies, and had been instructed by Ray Dallas to make no move unless he ordered it.

Mason said, in response to the statement Dallas had made, "Ray, the good fisherman will tell you that once you've baited your hook, you need patience to make your catch."

Dallas grunted. "I still hope you know what you're doing."

Suddenly, a whispered voice came over the walkie-talkie: "Lieutenant, there's a car coming in from the highway."

"Confirmed," Dallas said into his walkie-talkie. "Hold your positions. Stay alert."

Mason, peering through the foliage, saw the car stop a few feet away from the center of the clearing, but the car was too far away from him to identify the occupant.

Dallas was wearing a pair of binoculars by a strap around his neck. He raised the binoculars to his eyes and focused on the figure in the car.

"I'll be damned!" Dallas said softly.

"Who is it, Ray?" Mason asked.

Instead of answering, Dallas slipped the binoculars from around his neck and handed them to Mason.

Mason lifted the binoculars and saw Anne Kimbro in startling close-up, sitting in the car, staring out at the place where the house had once been.

Mason handed the binoculars back to Dallas. "Hold everything, Ray, until we see what she does now."

Anne Kimbro sat in the car for a long time.

"What's she doing?" Dallas asked softly. "Waiting for someone? Or maybe until it gets darker?"

Mason said, "Patience, Ray. Remember?"

He had hardly spoken the words before Anne Kimbro started up the car, turned, and drove away.

Dallas swore softly. "What do you make of that, Counselor? She didn't do anything we can arrest her for. Whatever you think this trap you've baited is, it hasn't caught her yet. If we question her, she'll say she just came out for a look at the place. What do we do now?"

"We wait," Mason said. "As you pointed out, maybe it has to get darker."

Dallas used his walkie-talkie to instruct the men to remain where they were.

They waited.

The last light of the sun disappeared.

The night was dark. There was no moon, and a light fog swirled in from the ocean. More time passed.

Again, sounding loud in the eerie silence, there was a whispered voice on the walkie-talkie: "Lieutenant, a car coming in."

Dallas repeated the same words of caution he had used earlier, when Anne Kimbro's car had been sighted.

Mason, watching, saw the headlights of a car as it came toward the clearing and stopped.

The car's headlights went out. A figure got out of the car and moved across the clearing to the stone chimney. In the fog and the darkness it was impossible to see more than that. The figure blurred into the shadow of the chimney.

Dallas used his walkie-talkie as the figure emerged from the shadow of the chimney and ran toward the parked car.

"Hit the searchlight! Don't let that car leave!"

The clearing blazed all at once with the harsh glare of the giant searchlights and, simultaneously, the blast of a fiery explosion that blew apart the towering chimney, hurtling chunks of stone upward and out through the trees.

Men were racing in from all sides of the clearing and had surrounded the car parked there.

Mason and Dallas moved quickly from the trees, and by the time they reached the car, several burly detectives had grabbed and were restraining the person who had set off the explosion and tried to escape.

Mason saw, with no surprise, that the man they were holding was Neal Granin.

Dallas pulled Mason aside.

"All right, Counselor, so we've caught Granin in the act of setting off an explosion—how's that going to enable us to charge him with murder?"

"For now," Mason said, "you're going to charge him with destroying evidence in a murder case."

Dallas looked puzzled. "Assuming that's true, and I'm not even sure it is, then what?"

"Walk with me," Mason said, leading Dallas away from where anyone might overhear them, and then saying, "while you're holding him on that charge, you're going to tell him how you're going to prove that he, not John Leland, murdered Iris Jantzen, and why he did it. You already have all the pieces of your case against Neal Granin. Now, you just put them together."

Dallas was frowning. "Go on."

"The murders of Elizabeth Jantzen and Iris Jantzen *were* always connected, although not because the same person murdered both of them. Benjamin Jantzen murdered Elizabeth *and* Edward Larner. We already know that. But Benjamin Jantzen didn't conceal Larner's body inside the fireplace along with the gun Jantzen used, with his fingerprints on it. Somebody else did that—Jantzen was busy at the time inducing the symptoms of a stroke so he couldn't be questioned by the police. We already know that. So you know somebody else had to have sealed up the body and the gun in the fireplace."

Dallas let his breath out. "Iris Granin, who later became Iris Jantzen!"

"Exactly!" Mason said. "Only she had help. The help of her teenaged brother, Neal Granin. And Benjamin Jantzen never knew what they'd done with the body—"

"And the gun with his fingerprints on it!"

"And the gun." Mason nodded. "Consequently, Iris had Jantzen right where she wanted him. Anytime he didn't do exactly what she wanted, she'd find a way to reveal the skeleton and the gun to the police."

"She blackmailed him."

Mason said, "She'd done it once before, blackmail, with a man named Harold Fadden, only she didn't get caught. I'll fill you in on the details later. For now, it's not important. In Jantzen's case, she blackmailed him into marrying her and cutting her in on the business, Questall Pharmaceuticals, which she more or less ran after Jantzen suffered a series of real strokes."

"Assuming all this is true," Dallas said, "how do I prove it?"

"As far as Neal Granin is concerned, you let him know about the incriminating clue against him, which is the reason he came out here tonight."

"What incriminating clue?"

"Before we discuss that," Mason said, "let's talk about the murder of Iris, and why Granin, and not John Leland, killed her."

Mason glanced toward the parked car in the clearing where Neal Granin was being held in custody.

"John Leland was telling the truth about that first phone call he received, asking him to come out here, where he met Anne Kimbro. Iris made that phone call, knowing that Anne would be here that day and that John would meet her. Iris probably read the same article in the papers that you read, rehashing the Larner-Jantzen murder. Then she went and checked the court records and found out Leland's new name. Of course, she couldn't have known that John and Anne would be attracted to one another when they met, and would fall in love. But she didn't necessarily need that to happen to fit into her plan. It would have been enough to be able to prove he'd been here at the house even once and had met Anne."

"Been enough to do what?" Dallas asked.

"To frame John Leland for Anne's murder after she, Iris, killed her," Mason said softly.

"Iris planned to murder Anne?"

"That's what it was always all about. That's why Neal Granin murdered Iris. He caught on to what Iris planned to do. Anne was going to inherit the business soon. I think Iris had been siphoning off money for herself all along, which would be discovered as soon as Anne inherited. Or at any time there had been an outside audit, as John Leland had suggested. Besides, even if Iris wasn't stealing for herself, she wasn't about to give up her catbird seat she'd worked so hard for and let Anne have it all. Iris was a scheming, ruthless person. On the day Iris came out here to the house, she thought Anne would be here, and she was going to kill her, then leave. She knew John Leland would be suspected of the murder, especially once it was discovered who he really was. You see, if you re- member, Anne was supposed to get here first that day.

Iris didn't know the plans had changed, and Anne was delayed."

"Wait a minute!" Dallas said. "Anne was delayed because Iris wanted her to pick up a cake."

"Anne was delayed," Mason said, "because Neal called her and *said* Iris wanted her to pick up a cake. Actually, Iris couldn't have known anything about it. Neal made that up because he knew Iris, knew what she planned to do, and knew there was no way to stop her unless he killed her himself. Which, after he followed her here, he did, and, incidentally, thought he was killing two birds with one stone, so to speak. Because he knew John Leland, who would be coming to the house after he left, after he had killed Iris, would be suspected of the murder—just as did happen. And Neal planted that left-handed gardener's glove to add to the evidence against Leland."

"Why would Neal Granin want John Leland out of the way?" Dallas asked.

Mason smiled. "For the same reason he wouldn't, couldn't, let Iris kill Anne. Neal Granin has been in love with Anne practically his whole life. They were always together before Leland showed up. I've seen nearly a lifetime of photographs of Anne and Neal together. And my hunch is, Granin expected and hoped to marry Anne himself in time, after John Leland was convicted of Iris's murder."

Dallas said slowly, "Well, it all hangs together, I must say. But I'm curious about this incriminating clue against Granin at the time Larner's body was concealed in the fireplace."

"Granin was in court today when I cross-examined Dr. Shuler, the DNA expert, on whether evidence, such as a hair, could still be tested even if there had been a passage of time since the evidence had been left at the scene of the crime. The doctor's answer was that testing could still be done, for example, on a hair, even if twenty-five years or so had passed—a time, I would remind you, longer than the years Larner's body was sealed in the fireplace by Iris and Neal Granin. The significance of the doctor's statement was not lost on Granin. Which is why he came here tonight to obliterate any possible evidence left around the place where they sealed up the body and the gun inside the fireplace that might have connected him to what he and Iris had done years before."

Dallas was thoughtful. "And it was Granin who burned down the house, too, so that eventually the skeleton and gun would be found?"

Mason nodded. "Yes. He wanted the skeleton found and Benjamin Jantzen known to be Larner's killer, because he wanted Jantzen out of the way, too. Either by suicide, which could have happened if Granin told Jantzen Larner's body had been found, or Granin could have killed Jantzen when John Leland called the house that day and said he was coming there. Granin could have seen his chance to kill Jantzen and make it appear that, again, Leland was the murderer. Whether you can prove Granin killed Jantzen is another case you can work on, after you've convicted him of the murder of Iris. Jantzen had to be eliminated because Granin couldn't be sure of what the old man might say about the part Iris and he, Granin, played in concealing the body. Remember, too, somebody tried to keep alive the illusion that Edward Larner was still alive after his body was stuffed into the fireplace. While John Leland was still a young boy, somebody sent money orders to the family from different cities. Iris, or maybe Neal, must have done that. Jantzen could have revealed it all."

Mason paused and then said, "Of course, Granin couldn't possibly have thought, before Dr. Shuler testified, that one of his own hairs recovered from the fireplace after all these years could, through DNA analysis, tie him to what he and Iris had done."

"Wait a minute!" Dallas protested. "If there was ever any possibility that there might have been evidence, a hair or whatever, left in the fireplace that could be linked to Granin, you've just let him blow it all to hell!"

Mason waved away the idea. "No. I took precautions against that happening. A couple of days ago I saw to it that all the stones and cement around the hiding place where the skeleton and gun had been sealed up were removed from the interior of the fireplace. If there was any evidence left behind, it's safe and can be analyzed. Drake has it ready to turn over to you."

"Did it ever occur to you that I could charge you with removing evidence in a murder case?"

"I hardly think so," Mason said. "If there was any evidence there, which, I might add, Forensic overlooked and failed to remove, all I did was take the precaution of keeping it in custody until I could turn it over to you."

Dallas shook his head. "I don't know what Carter Phillips would say if he knew about all this. . . ."

Mason smiled. "Oh, I don't think Carter Phillips need know about any of this. And he certainly won't from me."

Mason put his hand on Dallas's shoulder. "The way I see it, Ray, is, you confront Neal Granin with all you know. Plus the stones and cement he failed to destroy and that you are going to have sifted through for evidence that can be analyzed for his DNA. Then I'll bet," Mason paused and added, "that just telling him what you plan to do, along with your bulldog interrogation of him, he'll crack, and you'll have a confession by court time tomorrow. And all the credit. It's worth a try, wouldn't you say?"

"It's worth a try." Dallas grinned.

"And if you succeed"—Mason grinned, too—"you could always know this case was, one might say, won by a hair."

23

The courtroom proceedings the following morning were brief and dramatic.

Carter Phillips rose to ask Judge Maynard for permission to make an announcement to the bench.

After a quick glance at Perry Mason, who nodded, the judge said, "Very well, Mr. Phillips. Permission granted."

Despite the crowd of spectators packed into the courtroom, there was a hushed stillness as the district attorney spoke.

"Your Honor, the prosecution wishes to state that in the hours since this hearing was last in session, new evidence uncovered by the Los Angeles Police Department—and especially the brilliant deductive work on the part of Lieutenant Ray Dallas—has resulted in the solution of the murder of Iris Jantzen. The police have a complete confession from Neal Granin, admitting that he, and he alone, committed the murder."

"I have viewed the videotape of the confession," Judge Maynard said. "I am satisfied that the murder of Iris Jantzen has been solved."

"Therefore," Carter Phillips said, "the People move to dismiss all charges against the defendant, John Leland, in this hearing."

Mason spoke quickly. "No objection on the part of the defense, Your Honor."

Judge Maynard nodded. "The case against the defendant, John Leland, is dismissed, and he is free to leave forthwith. Court's adjourned."

Mason had always been intrigued by the actions of courtroom spectators, most of them strangers to the accused, who rushed forward—as now—to offer congratulations following an acquittal. Was it, he sometimes speculated, that they imagined themselves in the place of the defendant who had been set free? Was it that they had a need for justice to prevail? Was it simply that they wanted contact with someone they perceived as a winner against what they perceived as the odds? Or, perhaps, was it merely a ritual of informal celebration for the victor—as in all contests?

Mason moved away from the crowd surrounding John Leland when he saw Lieutenant Ray Dallas signaling to him, and the two met in an aisleway near the front of the courtroom. Carter Phillips had left hastily—no doubt, Mason supposed, to avoid talking to the news reporters.

Dallas said, "You must be feeling pretty good, Perry."

"I am," Mason admitted. "And so should you. After all, you did the hard work, getting Granin to confess."

"He was simply bowled over by all the evidence we threw at him," Dallas said. "I don't think it had ever occurred to him that anyone in the world would be able to figure out the intricacies involved in the two murders and put them all together. He verified everything you theorized about the two cases. In a way, I think he was glad to put an end to it all. The clincher, I believe, is that once he knew all we were going to offer as evidence against him, he knew he'd lost Anne Kimbro forever. Since to win her was why he had done it all, there wasn't much point in denying the evidence."

Dallas turned to go, then said, "There are a few loose ends to tie up yet. I want to see if we can recover any evidence from the debris from the fireplace to do a DNA analysis. And I still want to work on whether Benjamin Jantzen died or whether Granin killed him. But we have time on that one. Granin's not going anywhere for a while."

Dallas gave a wave of his hand and walked away.

Mason went over to where John Leland was still being congratulated by well-wishers. Della Street and Paul Drake were with Leland.

Leland grabbed Mason's hand and shook it, saying, "You did it, Mr. Mason! You did it!"

Before Mason could answer, another of the spectators had greeted Leland. Leland turned away briefly, but still gripped Mason's hand.

Mason looked at Della and Paul. "You two, we're taking the rest of the day and evening off. We're going to drive somewhere and have some champagne and dinner."

Della laughed. "It's a date."

Paul grinned and nodded.

Mason was aware that someone had taken his free hand and was holding it. He turned and saw it was Anne Kimbro. She stood on tiptoe and kissed him on the cheek.

"Thank you so much, Mr. Mason. I'm sad about Neal. I never suspected what he'd done."

Mason looked at her curiously. "Anne, what were you doing out at the remains of the house in the canyon last night? I was there. The police had the place staked out."

"I was just out driving, alone, trying to clear my mind after yesterday in court," she said. "And I drove there just to take one more look at what I hoped would be, finally, a closed chapter in my life. I had no idea anything was going on out there."

Mason nodded. "I thought it was something like that. And now, you can consider it a closed chapter in your life."

Anne had tears in her eyes. "Except for John. Do you think he can ever forgive me for doubting him?"

Leland was still turned away. Mason disengaged his hand from Leland's, removed Anne's hand as well, and joined Anne's and John Leland's hands together.

Leland turned then, and Mason said to Anne, "Why don't you ask him?"

Leland wordlessly pulled Anne toward him and took her in his arms.

Mason withdrew, leaving them like that. He joined Della and Paul, and they started out of the courtroom.

Paul said, "Perry, Cupid himself couldn't have brought two lovers together as well as you just did."

"Watch out, Paul," Mason warned, "I might just have another arrow in my bow, and if I aim it at you, it won't be at your heart."